INTO THE Hollow

Written by, Ethan Blake
Edited by, Laura Ann

authorHOUSE®

AuthorHouse™
1663 Liberty Drive
Bloomington, IN 47403
www.authorhouse.com
Phone: 833-262-8899

Published by AuthorHouse 07/27/2020

ISBN: 978-1-7283-6804-7 (sc)
ISBN: 978-1-7283-6803-0 (e)

Library of Congress Control Number: 2020913223

Print information available on the last page.

Chapter 1

October 30

A mother and her young daughter passed her by, their dark-rimmed eyes watching her, their paper-thin, pale skin casting them in a ghostly light against the rich amber glow of the setting sun. Amelia smiled nervously at them; but they only continued to watch her, slowing their pace, and turning to follow her. Whether it was due to the affliction that ravaged their bodies or the one that tormented their minds, causing them to take their own lives, the town had lost nearly half of its inhabitants. The fresh smell of rot lingered in thick, pungent clouds as rigor mortis slowly crept through town, not unlike Mary Shelley's inelastic reanimation of *The Modern Prometheus*.

'It's getting worse,' she thought.

The preacher, who had recently fallen ill, was standing in the doorway of the mercantile, blocking her entrance.

"Hello, Reverend Holcomb," Amelia said, barely able to contain the revulsion that welled up inside her and spread across her face from being so near to him.

"Will we be seeing you at church tomorrow morning, Amelia?" he asked as he held up his leather-bound Bible. His sunken eyes, as dark and hollow as the rest of the townspeople's, shuddered as they studied her.

"If you'll excuse me," she answered, avoiding his question and sidestepping his dark, towering figure to get into the store.

He only asked to make her uncomfortable; he knew she wouldn't be there. It had been months since Amelia had attended any type of church service, and she had no intention of returning to that awful place. A horde of seemingly mindless townspeople had formed both inside the store and outside, peering in through the rust-colored filth that had settled along the old glass windows. Their thin arms hung limp at their sides, their heads bent slightly downward; but their vacant, cold stares chilled her the most.

Distracted, Amelia reached for the bottle of ink on the top shelf; her nervous fingers fumbled through the cobwebs, causing her to nearly drop it. She quickly finished making her purchase and shuffled past the near immortuous spectators in the store. She didn't like their gloomy, grief-stricken eyes following her, making her the center of attention. She'd deliberately isolated herself from them. Part of her feared whatever contagion lingered in their bodies and swam through their blood, but more frightening was the possibility of what may have infected their souls.

The short walk from town to her house seemed longer than usual; and the orange, fiery glow of the setting sun cast long, eerie shadows that stretched on before her. It would be night soon, and she'd feel safer at home under the cover of darkness.

The night was calm and still; the pale, white moon shone softly through her bedroom windows. A noise roused Amelia from sleep. She quickly turned her head towards the sound, and was met by the shifting eyes of the pastor – two demented pools of rage that seemed to look right through her.

The reverend stood over her and frowned, his expression grim and guilt-ridden, his breath warm and foul as he leaned in close to her. "You will pay for your egregious sins, Amelia."

Her eyes widened in horror as she traced the dark outline of distant figures in the monochrome moonlight. Several of the townspeople stood behind him; and as he handed one end of a rough, frayed rope to another of the men, she watched his silhouette walk out her door, rope in hand. Instantly, she knew what they intended to do. Amelia felt the opposite end of the rope begin to constrict around her throat like a coiling serpent. She choked and let out a blood-curdling scream that was momentarily muted with each tug of the cordage.

The rope jerked once; she writhed in agony as she was violently yanked from her bed and dragged across the splintered wood floors of her home. Amelia frantically clawed at the boards and then the ground, breaking and ripping the nails from her fingertips in a useless attempt to get free. Her bloody hands pulled at the coarse rope around her neck as she gasped for air. As Amelia was dragged along the rocky soil, red dust kicked up around her in thick, heavy clouds, making it even harder to get air into her burning lungs. Bound behind the preacher's horse, her body twisted and bounced against the cold, unforgiving earth, the stones biting into her frail skin, leaving her with deep gashes and sharpened shards of bone protruding from her battered flesh.

The horse came to an abrupt stop, tossing Amelia's frail body to the side. She coughed and sputtered, spitting clots of blood and fractured bits of teeth into the dirt. She looked up through a thin film of her own crusted blood and foamy saliva. She peered through the blurry maze of jagged shadows cast by the crisp, autumnal moon and realized she had been dragged beneath the cover of the old, anfractuous oak tree that stood beside the rustic church. Spiritless people from town slowly traipsed by and gathered near a row of freshly dug graves to watch, to make sure she paid for what they knew she'd done. A handful of soulless, sadistic men put down their tarnished, brass-colored lever rifles and began to take turns having their way with her on the ground. Their complicit wives watched apathetically. Each man aggressively grabbed at her frayed hair, pulled at the tattered rope around her neck, and clung to her fractured jaw, forcing her to make eye contact while they violently thrust their way in between her bloody thighs. Reverend Holcomb stood opposite of the crowd in syzygy and diverted his weary eyes from the revolting assault. There was no need to restrain her arms or hold her legs apart; the tiny woman stood no chance of escape. Powerless, Amelia made one last attempt to struggle, to scream; but the only sounds she made were the high-pitched wheezes of a suffocating woman fighting for one last breath of air.

"No pleading or praying will save your soul, Amelia. Lives have been lost; lives have been taken! There is only one way to deal with a witch like you," the reverend said as he coughed up a thick yellowish-brown mucus, putting an end to the mindless torture in an effort to expedite Amelia's death. "Deliver me, my God, from the hand of the wicked, from the grasp of those who are evil and cruel."

The opposite end of the dark, bloodstained rope was thrown over one of the largest branches of the oak and then re-tethered to the preacher's horse.

As the horse slowly walked away from the tree, Amelia felt the slack in the noose disappear. As the preacher continued to cough up pools of bloody brown saliva, he pushed the horse forward. The townspeople watched, expressionless, in stoic silence. Step by step, inch-by-inch, the rope tightened around her neck, crushing her throat until her feet were slowly lifted from the ground. Dangling helplessly in the air, her toes stretched out, Amelia's blood vessels began to bulge and then burst behind her bloodshot eyes. The reverend stopped the horse, leaving Amelia's outstretched toes twitching only inches above the blood-soaked soil. Keeping her near this threshold of life and death seemed to bring the preacher's flock some sort of morbid sexual pleasure. In their minds, this torturous execution was not murder but a form of justice. The rope creaked and cracked as her body slowly swayed side-to-side. Amelia let out one final burst of violent convulsions and then went limp beneath the tree.

"Wait, they just raped her and then killed her?" Emerlyn asked, a look of absolute horror painted across her face.

Jack's father nodded. "Yes, but killing her didn't change anything. People continued to get sick, and die, even after Amelia was hanged. An unusually high percentage of the deaths were suicides; and because of that, some believed that with her final breaths, she cursed the wretched town."

Jack rolled his eyes. "Dad, we love Halloween and all, but that's an awful ghost story. Sounds pretty far-fetched to me."

"It's more than a story," Jack's father continued.

"What do you mean, Mr. C.?" Thomas asked.

The four nervously waited for his reply. All except for Jack who remained mostly uninterested in this particular type of hearsay as he sat with his arms crossed and a smirk painted across his face. Emerlyn felt a cool chill of unease as she rubbed her arms. She slid closer to Thomas, who cleared his throat and fidgeted with his glasses.

Jack's father smiled and kept his voice low as he resumed the tale. "Amelia was very real, as real as the oldest tree in the hollow that still stands near the ruins of the church. People say that on the days leading up to Halloween, the barrier between our world and the spirit realm grows thin, her soul becomes restless, and she is able to cross over onto our plane of existence. As long as she's left alone, there's nothing to fear; but," he paused, "if she is disturbed, they say she'll follow you through the hollow, attach herself to your soul, and wear away at your sanity until you are overcome with paranoia and the irresistible temptation of suicide."

Just then a strong breeze blew into the room, causing the window nearest Paige to slam closed. The girls screamed, and all four teens jumped. Jack's father laughed and took a sip of his Crystal Head Vodka. His mother entered the room with a cauldron shaped bowl of chips, set it on the kitchen table, and put a hand to her hip.

"What did you tell them?" she asked, squinting her eyes in Clint Eastwood fashion.

"Amelia's story," he answered, grinning. He paid no mind to his wife's intimidation techniques.

Jack's mother shook her head and walked to the window. She opened it and paused for a moment, staring into the twilight as though she were looking for something. "You really need to fix this damn window," she said frowning. Turning back to Jack's father, she continued, "And why the hell would you tell them about that? You know I don't like that disgusting story." This time her words were followed with wide eyes, her classic look of displeasure.

"Eh," he shrugged, taking another drink and slightly slurring his words. "They're old enough to know, Alice. Besides, tomorrow is Halloween, and it'll be their last one together before graduation! I figure they should hear one final, frightening folktale before they all move off to college, become boring, big shot executives, and forget all about our spooky little town."

"I object to the use of the word frightening in your description of the folktale, Dad." Jack shook his head and chuckled.

"What really made them do it?" Emerlyn asked quietly. Her eyes wandered around the room as a flood of uneasiness streamed across the back of her neck and trickled down her spine.

"Uh, they were all fuckin' insane?" Paige answered sarcastically. She giggled and leaned into Jack while secretly grabbing his inner thigh under the table. The sensation of fear worked like an aphrodisiac for the young couple.

Jack's mom sat down, trepidly smoothing the creases that had formed in her vintage pumpkin patch tablecloth. "Paige has a point. All it takes is a little common sense to figure out that it was likely some kind of contaminated food they all ate; the bread in the church is what most believe caused it," she continued. "It made the people hallucinate, even infected their minds to the point that it drove some to suicide. Since Amelia never attended, she never got sick. She became an easy target for their fear and paranoia. Besides, this tall tale is wrought with exaggerations. No more than a handful of the deaths were actually suicides, but a handful is more than enough." Jack's mother paused as a sad look crept across her face. "And to exacerbate the ignominy, they never even gave that poor girl a proper burial. Shameful."

"It's true," Mr. C. added. "As a teenager, I searched the hollow myself and never came across a headstone for anyone named Amelia."

"Well that's convenient, don't ya think?" Jack's voice was still painted with skepticism. "Just more small town bavardage as far as I'm concerned!"

"That's awful," Emerlyn said. She subconsciously reached for the cross that dangled around her neck and held it tightly.

"Yep, it's just so awful and very terrible," Jack agreed, giving his mother a look that signaled it was time for his father and her to leave the room. "But props to you Dad, because that was a super graphic ghost story! I'm pretty sure we're all scarred for life now." Jack awkwardly looked at his mother once more, his eyes begging her to take his father away.

"Come on, I think your stories have scared everyone enough for one evening." Jack's mother's tone became more serious, almost cautionary, when she continued, "Regardless of why Amelia was murdered, it's still an unforgivable atrocity and a stain on this town's history that shouldn't be told for the purpose of entertainment."

Jack's father stood up to leave and then paused before retreating to his den. "Just remember, whatever you do, stay away from that tree." Mr. C. winked at the kids behind his wife's back.

"That's the only sensible thing you've said all night," his wife interjected.

"Oh, don't you worry, Dad. We're all way too terrified to do something like that," Jack joked.

Thomas laughed nervously; he didn't want his friends to know how much the story had really affected him. He couldn't get the image of Amelia's dead body swinging from that tree out of his head; and the suicidal anomalies reminded him of a few other nightmarish "religious" groups.

Thomas's mind was always wrapped up in conspiracies and unexplainable phenomena. He thought back to the Heaven's Gate cult that committed a mass suicide under the Hale-Bopp Comet in '97, believing the comet was an extraterrestrial spacecraft that would escort them to the Kingdom of Heaven. Amelia's incident was different, though. It was way closer to home and so much more unnerving.

Jack reached into the black cauldron for some chips. "I've got an idea."

Paige grinned, Emerlyn grimaced, and Thomas tried his best to look enthusiastic. He knew that whatever it was, no matter how awful a suggestion, they'd go along with it. They always did. Jack's ideas were never good; and from his friend's expression, Thomas could tell this one was probably going to be terrible.

"We're going to that tree," Jack said.

"Oh my God, we have to!" Paige agreed.

"I don't know…" Emerlyn's brow furrowed. "Is that smart? I mean, it's a murder site."

"And technically also a suicide site," Thomas quickly added.

Emerlyn winced at the very thought of committing suicide. The word alone sent a sharp pain right through the pit of her stomach.

"Afraid you'll see Amelia?" Paige teased, drawing out the name Amelia in a pseudo- seductive tone that showed the dimples on either side of her face.

"Oh, fuck you." Emerlyn rolled her eyes. "Fine, I'll go, too. It'll be...fun."

But for a split second, her eyes met Thomas's; and despite her words, he saw her fear in them. He knew how she felt. His skin crawled, and the hair on his arms and neck stood on end as the words of Amelia's story replayed in his mind. Dread pooled in his gut as he thought about the old part of the forest, the hanging tree, the ruins of the old town, and the negative energy that probably still lingered there. Something sinister awaited them; and just because it was Jack who wanted to go, they'd all agree. He was a natural leader of terrible plans. One of these days, Thomas would get the courage to tell Jack that his plans sucked; but no matter how stupid he thought this idea was, he wasn't going to let Emerlyn go on her own.

"Thomas?" Jack asked semi-condescendingly, interrupting his thoughts.

"Sure, yeah. Let's go," he answered. His cellphone buzzed, and Thomas looked down at the screen. Max, his younger brother. He frowned, ignored the text, and quickly put the phone back into his pocket.

"Let me guess -- Max?" Jack asked.

Thomas nodded reluctantly and shrugged. "Yeah."

"You know what would be fun?" Jack grinned. "Bringing Max with us."

"Yes!" Paige exclaimed.

"I don't know..." Thomas hesitated. "He's kind of annoying. Plus, I don't think he needs to visit an old lynching tree."

Jack, continued in a sarcastic tongue, "Awe, come on. Tomorrow is All Hallows Eve. A little exploration of the occult never killed anybody. Plus, it's all horseshit anyway! Text him back; we'll pick him up on the way."

"Fine guys, but don't say I didn't warn you." Thomas rolled his eyes, sent a quick text, and his phone buzzed again almost instantly. He looked over at Jack with a hint of resentment. "He said he'll be ready. He also sent an eggplant emoji." Thomas sighed and shook his head.

Jack glanced in Paige's direction and grinned at the sight of her dimpled, sassy smirk.

"Hey, Ma! We're going to Thomas's house!" he called.

"You have to ask your father first," Mrs. C. yawped back from the hallway.

"Dad, we're going to Thomas's house, okay?" Jack yelled.

"Awe, leaving already? You guys are no fun! I was just about to tell you about the UFO foo fighters from World War II!"

"Bye dad..." Jack's voice trailed off as he and his friends scurried away, but Thomas secretly wanted to stay and listen to Mr. C.'s alien stories and watch Steve1989MREInfo sample military rations on Youtube.

With that, the group headed out into the cold, autumn night. Piling into Jack's brand new, black, four-door pickup, Paige eagerly slid into the front passenger seat, lifting the central console, quickly slipping her left hand under the steering wheel, and placing it back onto Jack's inner thigh. Emerlyn and Thomas passively shook their heads in disapproval and climbed into the back seat. Every street along the way was decorated for Halloween. Skeletons seated on porches awaited their guests, ghosts flew wildly in the breeze as they dangled from trees, and the illuminated faces of the jack-o-lanterns seemed to watch their every move. Kids, too excited to wait for Halloween night to don their costumes, scurried around their front yards like gaggles of little grotesque goblins and dusty, desert ghouls.

"This was always my favorite time of year," Paige said.

"Was?" Thomas asked, a perplexed look upon his face.

Paige shrugged. "Still is, except...my parents began using me as some sort of political pawn every Halloween since eighth grade. They're essentially whoring me around to creepy, old, rich people who are supposed to ensure the success of my future. Like, what the fuck does that even mean?!?" Paige's eyes began to tear up as she stared out the passenger window. "They refer to these Halloween gatherings as informal business meetings, but these corrupt senators and wealthy elites insist on bringing their underage daughters and nieces, forcing all of us to wear skimpy costumes for their viewing pleasure. They constantly try to get us drunk; I wouldn't be surprised if they've tried to drug us. I honestly can't count how many times I've been offered fuckin' DMT. Our guardians are completely complicit monsters!"

Thomas gasped from the back seat. "I knew it was basically a blackmail ball where people tried to take compromising photos of each other for leverage. I just had no idea it was this bad."

"It's so secretive and culty; anyone who tries to speak out against it ends up getting kicked out of office, fired from their job, or worse. There's really no escape." A teardrop rolled down Paige's cheek. "Hanging with you guys is my only sense of freedom. I really cherish our stupid, haunted adventures. Isn't it sad to think that going home is scarier than ghost hunting?" Paige looked over at Jack with sad, yet determined, eyes and a half-cocked smile. "But we'll have fun tonight. In fact, I demand that we have a great night together! Besides, like Mr. C. said, this is our last Halloween before graduation! We need this. I need this."

"Fuck, yeah," Jack said with a bit of arrogance in his smile, trying to ease the tension in the vehicle. He knew how much this time of year meant to Paige, and she knew that he'd do anything for her. If anyone ever really touched her, he'd kill them, no matter the cost. This night was important to everyone. Everybody had their own personal struggles and fears of the future, but it would all just have to wait.

Thomas and his family lived in an older subdivision. Flickering jack o'lanterns lined the dark, paved driveway, casting tangerine-colored light and charcoal black shadows that cavorted grotesquely across the faces of human skulls that lay scattered on the front lawn. It all reminded Thomas of the poem "Danse Russe".

Only one light was on in the living room, and Max was already waiting outside the front door. Adjusting the brim of his red ball cap, he grinned and waved when he saw the truck's blinding headlights pull into the driveway.

"Hey, Max," Paige said, half-flirtingly as he opened the door behind her seat.

"Hi, Paige," he said shyly.

Emerlyn slid closer to Thomas to make room. "Hi, Max. Nice hat."

"So, where are we going again?" Max asked, ignoring Emerlyn's compliment.

"We're gonna check out this creepy, old tree in the hollow that Jack's dad told us about," Thomas answered.

"Sounds pretty lame," Max replied, trying to impress the two girls in the truck with his dismissive attitude. "So what's the big deal with this tree anyway? There are trees everywhere. What makes this one so creepy?" Max paused and looked around. "Oh, and where'd you get this fancy, new truck, Jack? Did your mommy buy it for your big eighteenth birthday?" he teased and then laughed at his own joke.

Emerlyn and Thomas giggled at Max's questions as Paige gently pressed her elbow into Jack's ribs and winked.

As they continued towards the forest, they began to drop in elevation; and a thick blanket of ghostly fog appeared to patiently await them in the distance. The gritty grey of the paved highway abruptly turned into unplumbed potholes and neglected red dirt roads that weaved in and out of the hollow, becoming rougher, darker, and more heavily wooded. Jack smirked at the thought of finally showing off his truck's overlanding capabilities.

Thomas awkwardly interjected, "Do you even overland, Bro?"

Emerlyn snickered and leaned against Thomas as she tried to see out the window, noticing old, abandoned buildings in various stages of disrepair. Along the way, she'd seen a handful of shacks illuminated with oil lanterns instead of lights. She wondered if the buildings were currently occupied by residents or just horny teenagers looking for a place to screw around. Only a few storefronts remained, all of which had shattered windows, rusted metal signs, splintered porches, and had clearly been forsaken long ago. It made her think of a ghost town in those old Western movies. Only this time, there was the threat of an actual ghost.

"It shouldn't be too far from here," Jack said, turning onto a much narrower dirt road. Paige's dimples showed in the dim, blue glow of the dashboard as she smiled, leaned in close, and whispered her favorite lyrics about sharing a poisoned apple into his ear. Jack whispered back "Forever," as Breaking Benjamin began playing on the radio.

No sign marked the way to the hollow, and Emerlyn wondered if it had fallen down over the years or if the lack of markers was intentional. She tried to shrug off the unease, repeatedly telling herself to just have fun. Halloween was the time for going to scary places. *Besides,* she thought, *Max would be right. This would be pretty lame if we weren't at least a little scared.*

Scattered remnants of crooked fence posts, oxidized barbed wire, and unpaved driveways were the only indications that life had once existed here. Thomas adjusted his glasses and squinted as he peered into the darkness. He saw the hauntingly pale glow of moonlit headstones hiding beneath the fog. The sight alone sent a tingle of fear and excitement down the back of his neck. And the thought of it being so close to Halloween, well, it seemed to amplify all of his senses. Oddly enough, Thomas sort of liked the sensation of being afraid. He'd grown accustomed to the feeling while researching paranormal topics and various conspiracy theories.

"The trees are getting too thick. We're going to have to park and walk from here," Jack said as he brought the vehicle to a stop.

"I was afraid you'd say that." Emerlyn sighed while nervously adjusting the cross on her necklace.

Jack opened up the driver door and stepped out onto the rocky soil. "Hey, Babe, can you hand me my .357 revolver?" he asked while pointing under Paige's seat.

"Gladly," she replied with a sense of relief. "I was afraid you might have forgotten it."

"Now, you know me better than that, little lady." He chuckled while buckling the old leather gun belt around his waist. "And guys, careful getting out. Don't scratch my doors on any branches."

"It's really dark," Max whispered under his breath. Even the near full moon had trouble breaking through the massive tree canopy that towered above.

"Yeah, no shit Sherlock. That's why I brought a couple of these," Jack replied as he powered on a 1500 lumen flashlight and handed the other to Thomas. "We own the night! Let's go motha fuckas!"

Chapter 2

"Alright, guys, the only clues we have are from Dad's ghost story. We don't have trail maps or anything, so keep your eyes peeled for signs of any church remains, a burial ground, and, I guess, a creepy tree?" Jack couldn't help but laugh at the idea of a tree being scary. "The fog is starting to settle in, but I've the truck marked on my GPS. As long as we make it back to the truck, we've nothin' to worry about. Thomas, step down your flashlight output to a lower setting to conserve battery power."

As Jack led the group deeper into the hollow, the energy in the air began to shift. Max was noticeably less talkative, Thomas's posture became even more rigid and focused, Paige's eyes darted rapidly from one illuminated tree to the next, and Emerlyn had this unshakeable feeling of being watched.

Thomas dabbled in paranormal research, obsessed over ufology, and was well versed in cryptozoology. Unfortunately, all of these various hobbies and idées fixes were beginning to take a toll on his imagination. Supernatural thoughts of Amelia raced through his head. Every crackling leaf, broken branch, and shifting shadow cast by his flashlight seemed to have a mind of its own, and it felt like there was always someone or something just beyond the corners of his eyes. Perhaps Emerlyn's paranoia of being watched had influenced his thinking, but there was something even more terrifying weighing on Thomas's mind.

"What if there's still some sort of cult out here, guys?" Thomas muttered nervously. "I mean, we're all out here looking for an evil spirit and a cursed tree, but who's to say there aren't still some Charles Manson mother fuckers out here hanging people from trees? I mean, people all over the country do weird rituals in the woods. Haven't any of you seen the Bohemian Grove footage from Alex Jones?"

"Wait. Is that what we're looking for? A real ghost? That's fricken sweet!" Max exclaimed enthusiastically while looking at Thomas. "No worries, Bro. Jack's got his fancy cowboy gun with him. He can take care of those Charles Manson mother fuckers for you," Max continued, clearly teasing both Jack and his brother.

"Jesus, guys!" Emerlyn forcefully interjected.

"Yea, cut the shit, Thomas!" Paige replied.

"No, I mean, I think we're here." Emerlyn grabbed Thomas's flashlight and directed the beam through a patch of thick brush. Water droplets from the fog slowly drifted and twirled through the air like ghostly snowflakes. "I think there's an old clearing up ahead."

"How can you be sure?" Paige asked reluctantly.

Emerlyn looked back at Paige, "Because there's more undergrowth. That means…"

"That means these trees are younger!" Jack interrupted. "The older trees were cut down and cleared away."

"Probably to make room for a creepy death cult." Thomas sighed as he stared into the wraithlike rays of moonlight breaking through the clearing ahead. "I'm telling you guys, I have a bad feeling about this place."

Emerlyn carefully crept forward, her breath heavy and slow. Thomas reluctantly followed close behind, and Max somehow managed to sandwich himself between the two. With every step, Emerlyn meticulously moved each mangled branch from her path, bending them away and holding them until they were within Max and Thomas's grasp. Though he'd never admit it, even Jack felt a little on edge. He instinctively kept watch at the back of the line with Paige close by.

"Oh my God!" Paige exclaimed.

"What is it? Is everyone okay?" Thomas turned back toward them, eyes wide with fear.

"No! Everything is not okay, Thomas! I keep getting tangled up in these stupid, fucking branches," Paige retorted.

"Well, Babe, nobody told you to come out here in a Goddamn sundress," Jack answered sarcastically.

"It's not a Goddamn sundress, Jack." Paige knew he was being facetious. "This is serious Jack. The struggle is real."

Emerlyn ignored Paige's melodrama and held the course. "Ugh, guys,

I have good news; and I have bad news," she said, her manner and tone concerningly calm. "The good news is I think we made it to the clearing. The bad news is my flashlight is dying."

She pushed past the last tangled bits of undergrowth and peered across a seemingly endless meadow. As the light from her flashlight began to dissipate, she strained to focus, hoping that the shadow figure lurking at the corner of her eye was just another figment of her imagination. A heavier fog lingered there like a specter under the moon's cold gaze. Like a scene from *A Fire in the Sky*, a sharp beam of white light sliced through the thick atmosphere as Jack directed his flashlight to the front of the group.

Whether it was Thomas's paranoia or his nervous need to escape the claustrophobic feeling of the cluttered forest, the results seemed much of a muchness. Forgetting that he no longer had a flashlight of his own, Thomas feverishly scurried past the group. He found himself wandering blindly through the drifting haze. Then, there was a loud crash followed by an ear splintering, shriek!

Jack moved the beam of light towards the direction of the scream. "What was that? Is that you, Thomas?"

"Yea, it's me! Come quick! My leg is stuck!" Thomas let out a loud cough. "I fell through the ground or something. I don't know. Just hurry!" Thomas pleaded as he lay face first on the cold, rocky earth adjusting his glasses and continuing to cough up dirt.

Jack quickly darted through the ghostly curtain of fog towards the sound of Thomas's voice with Paige and the rest of the group following closely behind. "What the hell happened to you?" he asked, a rare, genuine tone of concern in his voice. "Are you ok, man? It looks like your leg is caught in some sort of wooden box or…"

"Holy shit! Thomas, your leg is jammed in a coffin! It looks just like Dracula's bed! I think I can see a real human foot sticking out, dude!" Max exclaimed as he ran over to his brother's side. "This is so cool! You know better than to go wandering off without us, Indiana Jones," he continued, masking the fear in his voice with a crooked grin in a failed attempt to sound brave in front of the girls.

Paige stood motionless at the foot of the grave, her right hand held tightly over her mouth. Emerlyn looked at Paige and followed the direction of her startled gaze until it was met with the face of a small dusty headstone that read:

"IN FILIAL REMEMBRANCE OF REV. HENRY HOLCOMB".

As Jack pried apart the brittle, broken box, Max pulled Thomas by the arm, dragging him through the soil until his lower body was no longer inside the shallow grave. The three boys dusted themselves off and peered into the open casket. All that was left was a faded, bluish fabric, a tarnished pocket watch, and the bones of an exceptionally large skeleton. As a strange, heavy energy filled the air, Thomas's midnight alarm indicated it was officially Halloween, and the boys wearily staggered away from the grave. Sensing the girls' uncomfortable silence, the boys directed their attention to the weathered headstone.

"Holcomb..." Jack whispered in disbelief.

"Our first clue from your dad's story," Thomas replied, a hint of dread in his voice.

"Anyone else have the feeling that we're being followed?" Paige asked reluctantly, a sudden tone of suspicion and worry attached to her voice.

"The second the flashlight started to fade, I swear I saw someone or something in my peripheral; but when I tried to look at it, it vanished. I just didn't think anyone would believe me if I said anything. I can't help but feel like it's Amelia," Emerlyn answered, her voice unintentionally shaky.

"I know exactly how you guys feel. Anatidaephobia is a real bitch!" Thomas exclaimed in the most serious of tones.

"Oh here we go again!" Max exclaimed, breaking rank in the line. "He's always going on these Goddamned rants about ducks and geese watching him. Thomas, Bro. I love you, but you need serious help!"

Jack pointed his light back at the headstone. "You guys are being ridiculous. Cut it out! There aren't any shadow figures, we aren't being followed by ghosts, we're not being spied on by ducks or geese, and Dad probably knew about this headstone inscription before he even told us the story. By the look of it, it has been here a pretty long time; but the dates are conveniently worn away, so this proves nothing." Even Jack had trouble believing his own words.

"I can't believe I'm saying this, but maybe he's right." Thomas said, swallowing the lump of fright that festered in the back of his throat. Secretly, though, he still feared the possibility of being watched by waterfowl from afar. "I say we press on to see what else we can find. This doesn't prove much about Amelia's story, and this will probably be our last Halloween adventure together. We should make the most of it. Jack should have plenty of battery power left in his light, we have our cellphones, and the truck is marked on the GPS. And if someone really is following us, we have the gun." Thomas looked over at Max with a confident look of reassurance, but Max knew his brother well enough to know when he was just trying to impress Emerlyn.

"Awe, come on! Just ask her out already. Geeze!" Max retorted, grabbing the bill of his ball cap and pushing his hair back with his other hand. "Everyone knows the real reason you want to be here. You only took off on your own because you're trying to be the hero. Just tell her you like her, Bro!"

Emerlyn understood the reference, but quickly changed the subject. "So what's next then?" she asked sternly. "We look for the church? For all we know it could be twenty-five yards away, and we wouldn't see it with all this damn fog."

"Well, for starters we could follow the old wagon trail," Paige said sarcastically as she pointed to the left side of the headstone.

Jack grabbed her hand and grinned. "Good eye, Babe! As long as we follow the trail, the moon should be bright enough to lead us in the right direction. I'll kill the light for a while to conserve battery. If we don't find anything in the next few minutes, we can turn back and call it a night. Stick close and just follow your feet."

The towering tree line that grew alongside the trail seemed to shapeshift into creepy, contorted silhouettes, like monstrous Skinwalkers lurking against the cold backlight of the moon. It was distracting, and Thomas found it difficult not to think about the shadow figures that Emerlyn mentioned. Maybe it was all just a simple case of pareidolia or maybe it was an omen, a warning not to go any further into this Aleister Crowley shit show. It all made Thomas feel so conflicted. At best, they would find proof that poor girl Amelia was murdered in the 1800s. At worst, they'd find out that the murders never stopped.

The old path was rocky, hard packed, and in surprisingly good condition. As the group followed their feet beneath the bleached glow of the moon, Jack was the first to spot the lone jagged outline of a large, twisty, tree-like silhouette just off the trail. He turned toward the rest of the group and reached into his pocket to retrieve the flashlight.

Emerlyn gasped, "Jack, flashlight. Now!"

"There's some sort of rubble here," Thomas whispered.

Jack nervously fumbled the flashlight in his hands, accidentally dropping it lens first onto the ground. "Dammit! I cracked the lens," Jack said with undertones of embarrassment. He frantically cleaned the debris from the bezel. "Still works though!"

Even with a fractured lens, it was easy to see that this insalubrious rubble was once a church of some kind. For whatever reason, it appeared to be vandalized. The bricks lay crumbled and scattered across a large raised foundation; at the far end, a tarnished crucifix dangled upside down from a partially intact stone wall. Several support beams had long since fallen and now laid sprawled out and splintered athwart the floor. There appeared to be an entrance to the cellar just behind the altar; but it, too, was in a significant state of disrepair. It would be nearly impossible to breach the basement door. No one made a sound. The headstone, the name Holcomb, the wagon trail, and now this church, it not only meant that Jack's father was telling the truth, but also that the tree where Amelia was murdered was unnervingly close by. Max had only heard bits and pieces of the story from his brother and friends; but his eyes started to water, not out of sadness but out of fear.

Suddenly, Jack recalled the distant silhouette; a nervous tick traveled through his bones in the form of pulsating chills. He anxiously turned the light in the direction of the dark figure and preemptively grasped the handle of his revolver, fearing that someone might be standing there, watching from within the shadows. His father's stupid ghost story was becoming all too real. In near perfect unison, the group's eyes followed the beam of light until it revealed the base of a large oak tree, its lower limbs twisted and tangled beneath the cold October sky. Its sickly roots weaved in and out of the ground and under their feet like a malevolent hand of Hell extending an open invitation; and its leafless branches poked and prodded the thick atmosphere like the covetous fingers of demons desperately reaching towards the heavens. On cue, the pale, soft glow of the moon began to shift into a harsh hue of blood red. Everyone noticed it, but no one said a thing. In that moment, Max knew that everyone else had tears in their eyes, too.

"Ok, we found it. Now we can go, right?" Paige quietly begged Jack as she grabbed his arm for a sense of security.

Emerlyn put her hand on her chest, reaching for her crucifix necklace in an attempt to find her own feeling of safety. Thomas and Max stood closer together than usual.

"We can go, Paige. We just have to prove that we were here first," Jack said as he carefully navigated through the minefield of mangled roots. "We can't have any of our classmates out here claiming our territory!"

"What? Why does that even matter, Jack?" Paige asked, a deep sense of pleading in her voice.

"Every All Hallows Eve we try to up the ante, something bigger and better than the year before. We're a little early this year, but this is it! This is probably the scariest place we'll ever go! Just trust me. We'll be out of here in no time." Jack continued to approach the trunk of the old oak, as the group intentionally slowed their pace. The enmeshed branches above cast a series of sinister shadows across their faces, and the crimson glow of the moon washed over them like waves of blood in an ocean of dread. "Here, Thomas, hold my flashlight. Shine it steady so I can see." Jack handed him the light and put his hand on the tree, running his fingers across its many unusual scars.

"Do you guys hear that creaking sound?" Emerlyn asked as she looked up into the tangled web of branches, half-expecting to see a nest of demons.

"Relax, Em. It's an old tree. Old trees make noises," Jack said dismissively as he continued to examine the tree's excessive scab-like markings. In truth, he was scared shitless, but that was half the fun of it.

"But there's no wind," Thomas added as his hands began to shake.

"Can you please hold the light still?" Jack riposted as he reached into his back pocket and pulled out a Dalton Cupid automatic knife.

"What are you doing with that?" Paige asked. Ignoring the question, Jack drove the tip of the blade through the outer layer of bark and began carving his name.

"Just relax, Babe. I'll be done before you can say 'knife'," Jack smirked.

"Are you serious right now, dude? You really think you should carve Jack & Paige on a tree where a girl was murdered?" Max asked in disbelief.

"I mean, do you, be you, and just live a little, I guess..." he joked to ease the tension.

"You better not put my name on that Goddamn tree, Jack! Stop fucking around. I wanna get out of here," Paige commanded. "This isn't fun anymore!"

"Guys, the creaking. It's getting louder." Emerlyn's voice shook as she continued to stare into the branches.

"I hear it, too," Thomas said, moving closer to Emerlyn.

"Me, too," Max agreed.

"Look, guys, I'm done. Doesn't that look nice, Paige?" Jack asked with a smirk.

"Yeah, really fuckin' sweet, Jack-ass," Paige answered only half-sarcastically.

"One more thing," Jack said. He tossed his phone to Thomas and pulled Paige closer. "Take a photo of us in front of this beautiful work of art. It's all the proof we'll ever need, but back up a little. Try to get most of the tree in frame."

"Thomas, just hurry up and take the damn picture so we can get out of here," Paige pleaded.

"Ok," Thomas replied as he slowly backed away from the tree. He did his best to hold the flashlight steady in one hand and get the tree's lower branches in frame with the other hand. "There. All done! We can go now!"

"Well, not without me proofing the photo first," Jack said as Thomas tossed the phone back to him.

Jack and Paige looked down at the photograph on the phone, and she instantly emitted a bone chilling shrill of horror. Jack instinctively grabbed her by the arm and screamed, "Run!"

Without hesitation, the group bolted across the vein-like roots, down the wagon trail, and through the meadow. The faulty flashlight flickered through the fog as Thomas frantically fled from the creaking tree. Jack tore through the brush at the tree line, slicing his hand wide open on thorns. He only glanced at the GPS for a general sense of direction. None of them really cared where they were going. All that mattered was that Jack and Paige saw something horrifying in that photo, and everyone's nightmarish imaginations were running wild.

"There! Right there!" Jack exclaimed, pointing at the outline of his obsidian truck against the rose-colored sky. Everyone militaristically piled into the vehicle and locked the doors. As they fishtailed away from the trailhead, the black shine of the truck shimmered underneath the luminescence of the bleeding moon above.

"Jack, your hand!" Paige attentively examined it.

"It's fine," he answered dismissively.

"What did you see? What's in that photo?" Emerlyn asked.

Jack held the phone in his injured hand. "Look for yourself."

As Emerlyn reached for it, Paige started crying softly in the front passenger seat. Thomas and Max reluctantly leaned into Emerlyn, terrified but curious to see the picture. Once more, that old familiar chill was accompanied by tear-filled eyes. There they were, standing on either side of the tree. An ebony sap seemed to ooze from the carving: Jack & Paige. Emerlyn began to breathe heavily as she forced her hand over her mouth and turned away from the phone. Thomas grabbed it from her and adjusted his glasses while Max just stared emotionless into the darkness. There was something else in the photo. Thoughts raced through their minds: the creaking sounds, the red sky, Emerlyn's shadow figures, the church, the grave, all of it. On the right side of the photo, just beside Paige, was Amelia. Her neck twisted and dislocated, her lifeless eyes bulging from her disfigured skull, splintered bones protruding from her battered flesh, and fresh blood pooling from her inner thighs, there she hung.

Chapter 3

As Jack and Paige pulled up to her driveway, he noticed the long, orange curtains in the windows were lined with voluptuous Halloween decorations, clear indicators that her parents were preparing for their annual self-serving political gathering. It wouldn't be complete without their mandatory vampire facials, of course. Jack remembered the look of horror that remained painted upon Thomas's face the whole ride home. The scene before him was very reminiscent of Thomas's Bohemian Grove remark and all of the other occult rituals practiced by these weirdo elitists. It was becoming more and more obvious that this town held some very dark secrets. Jack had the terrible habit of ignoring Thomas's rants and raves; but sometimes he listened and even shared some of the same fears, especially when it came to Paige's involuntary involvement.

He stared at Paige with a deep longing in his eyes, begging for her to stay in the truck. Every fiber of his being was screaming for her not to grab that door handle. The sight of her there, sitting next to him with torn clothes and teary eyes, made him want to protect her. Instead, it seemed he was handing Paige over to two of the most unloving parents of all time. They'd rather whore their daughter around for the promise of power and money than spend a single moment acting like real human beings. Paige sat farther away from Jack than usual. Her body language indicated that she placed most of the blame on Jack for the night's horrifying sequence of events. Her eyes remained fixated on his phone as it lay face down on the dashboard.

"No one's going to believe us, ya know? The whole idea was just stupid. Even with a picture of us in front of that fucking tree with our Goddamn names carved into it, no one will believe us," Paige's voice cracked as she continued to stare at the back of the phone, her eyes filling up with tears.

"We can't even show the photo to anyone. There are apps that can do that sort of thing. People are going to tell us we're liars and that she isn't real. They're going to say the photo was digitally altered or photoshopped or whatever! So please tell me Jack, what the fuck was the purpose of any of it? What were you thinking? Amelia, that thing. . .It's going to find us. Thomas knows it. Emerlyn knows it. Hell, we all know it! Your father warned us!"

Jack's eyes watered with regret, but she never looked up. What could he possibly do or say in a situation like this?

Paige reached for the door handle, opening it slowly, "I just hope your dad was wrong about Amelia following us home to finish the job."

She stepped out of the truck and trudged towards her front door, and Jack couldn't help but notice that the color of the moonlight had returned to its normal cold, white glow. It was the perfect lighting to match the cold shoulder that he was getting from Paige. As she continued into the house and closed the door behind her, Jack began to feel the sharp pain in his hand that was previously masked by shock and adrenaline. He looked down. It was much worse than he remembered. The primary cut was deep inside the palm of his right hand, revealing a yellowish layer of fat lined with dirt and clumps of clotted blood. He threw the truck in reverse and slowly backed out of Paige's driveway, secretly hoping she would come running back. He knew better, but still he felt his soul screaming out to hers.

On the way home, thoughts started swirling around Jack's head. He found himself looking in the back seat through his rearview mirror, half expecting to see Amelia's mutilated corpse behind him. It felt like she was there, and maybe she was. After all, no one seemed to see her dangling from the tree until after the photograph was taken. Was she there all along? Emerlyn seemed to think so.

"God, I'm such a fucking idiot! I should've listened to Emerlyn. She told us that she kept seeing a shadow figure. She explicitly said that she somehow knew it was Amelia; but more importantly, I should've listened to Paige. No wonder she's pissed. I never listen." Jack checked the back seat again, let out a long exhale, and noticed the time on his dashboard display. "Well, it's nearly 3 am, the witching hour. Happy Halloween, Paige," he whispered in the darkness.

Jack parked his truck in the garage next to his father's rusted workbench and immediately began sifting through the first aid kit at the sink. He grit his teeth and poured alcohol straight into the open wound, trying desperately not to yell from the surge of throbbing pain that shot straight through his hand. "Shit, shit, shit. Fuck!" Jack quietly yelled into his left hand. He didn't want to wake his parents. If his mom found out what happened, she'd either have a nervous breakdown or divorce his father for telling that damn ghost story in the first place. Regardless, it was best to keep this whole thing a secret.

He snuck into the house to finish cleaning up, carefully wrapped his wound in gauze, placed his everyday carry items on the nightstand, and laid down on his bed. The cold sheets seemed to temporarily alleviate his aches and pains. Normally, he'd call Paige to wish her goodnight; but in all honesty, it wasn't a good night. It was a horrible night, and Jack had no desire to look at his phone. It had that thing on it, and its energy was so heavy.

Over the course of the night, Jack began to feel a great weight settle upon his shoulders; more than that, he felt it in his soul. Was it fear, confusion, and guilt all mixed up and intertwined? Whatever it was, it was nauseating yet numbing. It felt like a riptide of negativity and paranoia had washed over his psyche and slowly dragged his sanity out to sea.

Not long after he closed his eyes and drifted off, Jack heard a light tapping on the bedroom window. At first it was barely audible. Then, it grew louder and louder until it was apparent to him that it was more than just the wind. He grabbed his gun off of the nightstand and slowly approached the window from the side, cautiously peeking through the gap between the curtain and the wall. In spite of the abundance of ambient light outside, Jack could only make out the silhouette of a girl with long hair. He thought about grabbing his flashlight; but he knew if it was Paige, she'd kick his ass for shining that damn thing in her face. Besides, he was already in hot water with her. And honestly, who else could it be?

Jack opened up the window as the figure slowly backed away, motioning for him to follow. "Paige? Is that you?" he asked as he climbed out of his window. "Goddammit, Paige. What are we doing here? It's late." He continued to follow the girl around the side of the house until they reached the garage where his truck was parked. "Oh, I get it. You just wanted a little more privacy? Is that it?" he asked, but still no reply. Jack followed her through the side entrance of the garage. The door was already open, and it was dark inside. "Hang on, I'm going to hit the lights," he announced aloud, half-talking to himself.

"No lights," the girl softly replied. It was at that moment that Jack felt a swell of relief come over him. The voice sounded just like Paige.

"Ok. We can leave them off, but the cab light is going to turn on once we open the doors, silly," Jack giggled. He knew he'd never fully understand Paige or any woman for that matter. He was completely aware of that fact. Even still, he found her actions humorous at times. Jack watched her crawl into the passenger seat as he walked around the back of the truck, approaching the driver's side. He opened the door and noticed that she was looking away from him. "What are you looking at?" he muttered nervously. Still, there was no reply. "Look, I get it. You're still mad. I fucked up bad tonight. I never should have pushed things that far. I know that you had my back the whole night. You agreed to go to the stupid hollow and chase some dumb ghost story with me, and I just went way too far with the whole thing." As the cab light faded, Jack placed his revolver on the dash, resting his forehead on the steering wheel. He stared at his bandaged hand. "Paige? Could you talk to me? I'm sorry." He turned to look at her, but her darkened silhouette was still gazing through the passenger window.

"Start the truck. I'm cold," she muttered as she peered into the darkness.

"I really don't think that's a good idea, Paige. If I wake my parents and they see you here this late, they are going to lose their shit!" He felt her grab his inner thigh while slowly creeping across the passenger seat. As she lay her head down on his lap, he felt the chill of her long hair falling across his knee.

"Please, Jack? I'm so cold," she whispered softly into his waist.

Against his better judgment, he reached for his spare key in the visor and cranked the truck. The headlights blasted the white walls of the garage with a powerful surge of light, momentarily blinding him. When his eyes finally adjusted, he put his bandaged hand on her shoulder and looked down to see her face. He longed to see some sort of forgiveness in her eyes. Paige meant everything to him. Only, it wasn't Paige.

Jack looked down to see a face so disfigured, so inexplicably marred, that his mind could not fully process it. There were no horror movies, special effects, or photos of cryptid creatures from Thomas's collection that could have ever prepared Jack for the thing that was looking up at him. The only word running through Jack's mind was inhuman. With his off-hand, he instinctively reached for the double-action revolver on the dash, pointing it down, and squeezing the trigger. As the hammer pulled back and the cylinder rotated, the figure looked into the barrel and laughed hysterically with eerie polyphonic overtones. Its putrid tongue stretched out far beyond its decaying, needle-like teeth; and its hands began to grab and pull at Jack's groin in an overtly perverse manner. The hammer traveled forward and struck the bullet's primer. There was a flash of orange light, an excruciatingly loud bang, and then silence.

Jack opened his eyes. There was no figure, no entity, nothing inhuman digging its nails into his genitals. There was only blood, pools of it. And that same thick, yellow fat that he saw from his hand wound was now bulging out of the bullet hole in his thigh. Jack's leg was split open like an overripe pomegranate. The bullet had narrowly missed his near-mutilated genitals. As the deafening silence turned into a high-pitched ringing, he attempted to scream, but the tornado of pain, confusion, and the pungent smell of his own blood was so overwhelming that he lost consciousness. Jack was quickly bleeding out behind the steering wheel of his truck, alone.

Chapter 4

It was late. The clock had just struck midnight, and Thomas was distracting himself with another virtual reality horror game. Maybe it was a simple case of nyctophilia, but he found a certain level of comfort in scary games, especially the ones that involved Bigfoot. It was officially Halloween; and anything was better than thinking about that damned photograph on Jack's phone, much less the traumatic experience of falling into Reverend Holcomb's grave. It was difficult for Thomas's mind to sort it all out. When he was online, he could be anybody he wanted and go anywhere his heart desired. Right now, his heart desired to be as far away from the hollow as possible.

Thomas put on his VR headset and joined his friends' online party. Together, the three of them would be tasked with tracking down the Bigfoot creature, tranquilizing it, and bringing it back to base camp for scientific analysis. A loud Sasquatch howl in the distance sent serious shivers down Thomas's spine. The cratered moon above cast jagged shadows across the virtual Redwoods forest floor. He and his friends began to giggle nervously, and the game was underway!

In spite of being fully immersed in the game, Thomas couldn't shake the feeling of being watched in his room. His mother was on another graveyard shift, and Max was in the shower; so why did it feel like someone was watching him? Was it Amelia? Did she follow him home? In the middle of his thoughts, Thomas felt a light tap on his left shoulder.

"Hey. Thomas, can you hear me?"

Thomas bolted through the dark of his room with lightning speed, threw his headset onto the floor, and frantically flipped on the lights.

"Whoa, whoa, whoa…Easy there cowboy," Max sarcastically put his hands in the air to indicate that he was surrendering to Thomas.

"Max! What are you doing in my room? You scared the shit out of me!" Thomas's words trembled as he rested his right hand across his chest to feel the heavy thud of his racing heart.

"Now, that's no way to treat someone who's giving you a gift," Max smirked.

"Gift?" Thomas replied with a hint of suspicion in his voice.

"Yea, so you know how you took off across the meadow like a maniac and fell into that super creepy grave?" There was an uncomfortable moment of silence as Max stared blankly at Thomas, still struggling to catch his breath. "Rhetorical! Don't answer that! Of course you remember. I mean, how could you not? It was like a few hours ago, and super creepy..."

"Max! Could we not talk about it?" Thomas interjected.

"Well, that's going to be sort of impossible after I give you this gift," Max muttered nervously.

"And why is that?" Thomas narrowed his eyes.

"Well, I kind of thought you might want a souvenir from our little ghost adventure tonight. But that was totally before all of that real ghost stuff happened, so I forgot that I had it in my pocket," Max slowly began to feel a sense of regret swell in his throat.

"Had what in your pocket? Spit it out already, Max!" Thomas commanded.

Max slowly handed Thomas an old leather-bound book and said, "I found this in that Holcomb dude's grave. After Jack pried open the coffin and I dragged you out, I saw that book chillin' under the guy's arm. It was covered in some serious crud, but I cleaned it for you."

"You mean you robbed a grave? Max, what were you thinking?" Thomas pleaded for a logical response.

"Well Thomas, when you put it that way, it makes it sound kind of bad!" Max shifted his eyes to the floor in embarrassment.

"That's because it is bad, Max!" Thomas quickly examined inside the front cover and instantly recognized what it was. "You stole a dead man's Holy Bible. That's just great." Thomas was genuinely upset with his brother, but his curiosity currently outweighed his concern. Thomas continued to gently thumb through the fragile pages, noticing various inscriptions apparently handwritten by Reverend Holcomb. As he reached the final few pages, Thomas's face shifted to its signature look of horror, and Max immediately knew something was very wrong.

"What is it? What do you see?" Max asked reluctantly.

"Did you read any of this, Max? It's about Amelia." Thomas's hands began to shake as he read from the book.

> "I've seen what that cursed book and its perverse teachings can do in the hands of a foolish sinner. I've taken great care to bury the wretched grimoire alongside the remains of its last suspected user, Amelia Groeh. My attempts, however, did not satiate the Devil's hunger. Death is upon me. The tomb was disturbed, and the spellbook is missing. As I feel the affliction taking over, I am left to wonder whether or not I am the foolish sinner who lent his hand in the execution of an innocent girl in the name of false accusations. Or has Amelia Groeh truly transcended Death and risen from the very grave that I dug with my own two hands? God, deliver us from Evil."
>
> -Henry Holcomb

Thomas continued to hold the book open to Reverend Holcomb's last entry, contemplating its meaning and fighting the continual soirée of tremors in his hands. "There's a grimoire."

"A grim-what? What does that mean?" Max's eyes supplicated Thomas for an answer.

"It's a book of spells, magic, and instruction," Thomas replied in a dreadful tone. "It means there's more to Amelia Groeh's story than we've been told. Unfortunately, it also means we might have to go back to the hollow."

"Back to the hollow! Are you out of your freakin' mind? You're the last person on Earth I'd expect to say that!" Max retorted, feeling overwhelmed.

"As much as I don't want to talk about it, terrible things happened in that place." Thomas closed Holcomb's Bible. "If what the reverend said is true and there's witchcraft involved, we might be cursed for disturbing the grounds, especially if it has anything to do with this Bible or that creepy tree. Believe me. I've read many books on witchcraft, demonology, and dark energy. We do not want to mess around with this stuff. We need to know what we're dealing with and make damn sure we put Holcomb's Bible back where it belongs."

"No way, Bro! I'm not going back to the hollow tonight!" Max replied sternly.

"Fuck that! I said we had to go back. I never said anything about going at night! We'll convene with the others in the morning. You have to return this holy book to its rightful owner. Who knows what kind of energy is really attached to this thing." Thomas handed the book to Max and frowned.

"And all of this on Halloween? That's just fuckin' great!" Max detested.

Chapter 5

Halloween Day

Emerlyn opened her bedroom window to get some fresh air. As the fiery morning star slowly edged its way over the horizon, it seemed to set the sky aflame. She breathed in the cool, crisp air and felt the familiar sting of the sun's rays touching her face as she bathed in a shower of oranges. The soothing sun simmered in stark contrast to Emerlyn's cold gaze. She had not slept a wink, and her movements were slow and stiff like a Haitian Voodoo Zombie.

As Emerlyn slowly turned from the window, a part of her thought this might be a glimpse of heaven or purgatory or whatever happens after life. She half-expected Death to come for her during the dark of night. Instead, she crept across the cold floor with acute tunnel vision, shaking at the thought of what might lie on the other side of her bedroom door. It was the only way to get to the bathroom, and she'd been holding her pee all night out of fear.

She turned the knob and opened the door, the heavy hinges letting out the kind of spine-tingling screech you'd come to expect from a run-of-the-mill horror movie. It just so happens that stereotypical sound is much scarier in real life, especially now.

The hallway was still dark, obnoxiously dark. Make a right, and she'd be in the living room with plenty of natural lighting but no bathroom. That would be too easy. As luck would have it, Emerlyn had to wander a little farther into the darkness, a little closer to that creepy room that stood so menacingly at the end of the hallway. The one that she was never allowed to enter. The very space in which her grandmother used the edge of a rusty razor blade to slit her wrists after the doctors told her the chemo treatments were no longer working. Emerlyn would never forget the way her bloody arms hang from either side of the old rocking chair or the sight of her white wig lying on the floor in a pool of her own cold blood. Since that unspeakable act of grief and desperation, the house's ambient light never seemed to penetrate the darkness that enveloped the door frame. Even now, Emerlyn knew there was a room there but could only see pulsating splotches of black. Perhaps it had something to do with her tunnel vision, but even Thomas would say there was a certain tenebrosity about it. They were often in agreement about such things, even without speaking much to one another. Words were overrated and frequently unnecessary, anyway.

After what seemed like an eternity of zombie-like hobbling, Emerlyn finally made it to the bathroom. As she flipped on the light switch and sat down on the cold toilet seat, she noticed her reflection in the large rectangular mirror, opposite of her. She looked a little worse for wear. Not only was she sleep deprived, but her body took a serious beating while running through the hollow. Ruptured blood vessels left black and blue pigments peppered across her skin, and her limbs were lined with dozens of tiny abrasions.

She sighed, "I guess those branches and briars weren't quite as forgiving as I'd imagined. That would explain the stiff, achy muscles and tunnel vision."

Emerlyn flushed the toilet and looked back into the mirror. Suddenly, her reflection seemed less familiar, more like a complete stranger. It was as if the young woman in the mirror was really staring back at her, staring with a look of pleading and horror. The image began to pulsate as Emerlyn warily approached the sink to wash her hands. Her head was throbbing from an incessant migraine, so maybe these distortions of reality were all somehow related. She cupped her hands under the faucet and splashed cold water on her face.

"Maybe this will help," she thought aloud.

Emerlyn reached for the hand towel on the right side of the sink and turned off the water. As she buried her face in the fluffy cloth, she noticed how unusually silent the house had become. Once more, she looked into the mirror, removing the strands of wet hair from obstructing her view. Only this time, Emerlyn looked deeper. She leaned closer. The harder she stared, the less she recognized the girl leering back at her. Her wrinkles looked deeper, her hair darker, and the blue of her irises seemed to grow thin behind dilated pupils. The rope necklace that she wore began to look more and more like a noose. Each drop of water dripping from the leaky faucet seemed quieter than the last. Until it all faded into a distant thrum.

Emerlyn snapped out of the hypnotic trance of the mirror and slowly opened the door. She stepped into the dark hallway, her eyes purposely avoiding the direction of her grandmother's bedroom. She didn't have to look that way to know something was there. She felt it. There was a heavy presence, the kind that never leaves. As she turned toward the living room, she felt a chill crawling across the small of her back. It felt like the ice-cold fingers of Death reaching for her, lightly tugging at her shirt. Against every natural instinct in her body, Emerlyn turned around and stared into the bewitching abyss.

There was a creaking sound. It was hauntingly familiar. It wasn't like the sound of the squeaky door hinges in her room. No, this was distinct. This was rhythmic. With each creak and crack, Emerlyn took a step closer to her grandmother's room. She strained her wild eyes in the darkness, but could not see the door. Mesmerized and terrified, Emerlyn continued down the long hall with her hands stretched out, appearing even more like a zombie than before. Finally, she felt her trembling hands touch the cold brass of the doorknob. Emerlyn gently put her ear to the door, half-expecting the creaking sound to stop. Instead, it persisted.

Still in a trance-like state, Emerlyn slowly turned the doorknob and carefully opened the door. The room was pitch black, but there was a faint bit of light still emanating from the far corner where her grandmother taped the shade to the window. She remembered how sensitive her grandmother had become to sunlight after the cancer.

She fumbled her hand along the wall, her fingertips begging to find the light switch. Creak. Crack. Creak. Crack. The sound continued. Once again, Emerlyn found herself staring into the abyss, and at that precise moment, she knew that the abyss was staring back at her.

A wave of burning sensations rushed across her scalp, through her face, and down her chest as her eyes adjusted to the faint bits of light bleeding from the window's edge. Emerlyn saw the outline of her grandmother's old chair as it rocked back and forth amidst the shadows. Creak. Crack. Creak. Crack. Her eyes filled with tears, just as they did when she first saw the tree in the hollow. Flashes of the shadow figure, the forest, the church, and that photograph on Jack's phone played through her mind like an old film reel. Each image was grainy, the edges slightly distorted, and reminiscent of her hometown's dark past. In that moment, everything felt wrong. This didn't feel anything like her grandmother's energy. It felt older but familiar. This was shunning yet inviting, begging for attention in isolation.

Too terrified to turn around, Emerlyn instinctively backed away from the room and into the hallway. The chair began to slow its pace until the creaks stopped, and there was a forceful thud. Was it the sound of a heavy footstep? Emerlyn wondered. Whatever was in that room, it took notice of her, and now it was following her.

"Amelia?" Emerlyn whispered under her breath. She felt a strong hand grip her shoulder and forcefully tug her out the room and into the hallway.

"Emerlyn, what the hell are you doing? I thought I told you this room was off limits!"

"Dad?" Emerlyn mumbled through her tears.

"Em, what's gotten into you? You stay out all hours of the night. Then, you come home with bumps and bruises all over your body. And now this? You know your mom and I forbade you from ever entering this room! There's too much negative energy in here."

"I know, Dad. I'm sorry." Emerlyn sniffled and watched helplessly as her father quickly closed the door to her grandmother's room.

"Now, come with me to the living room, Em. Your mother and I need to have a talk with you."

Emerlyn did her best to collect herself before entering the living room. Truth be told, she felt a bit like Alice in Wonderland. Her mind was busy spinning derisory thoughts around her head like tiny little spiders, weaving figments of her prodigious imagination in and out of her own miniscule reality, tethering them together until the boundaries between the two were indistinguishable. It was getting harder and harder to tell the difference between her world and the spirit realm. Emerlyn shut her eyes tightly. She wondered if anyone else caught a glimpse of the apparition lurking just behind the living room curtains.

"Listen Em," her father spoke softly as he sat next to her mother on the couch. She, too, had tears in her eyes, but Emerlyn had no idea why.

"Mom. Dad. What's going on?" She felt a rush of panic dart across her chest. Her father's eyes were tense, and the tone of his voice was overly soft. Both were obvious signs of bad news lingering behind his lips.

"Em, your mother and I received a call from Jack's parents this morning." Her father's voice started to crack a little. There was a familiar sound of sadness embedded within his words. "Listen, people do these things in times of desperation. You know how much your grandmother struggled. It's no one's fault..."

"Dad, spit it out! What happened?"

"Baby Girl, Jack's mother found him locked inside of the garage. His father thought he heard a gunshot in the middle of the night. He went room by room with a pistol but didn't find any intruders. When he got to Jack's room, he noticed that Jack was missing, and his window was open. At first, they suspected that he snuck out with Paige. Then, his mother heard the truck idling inside of the garage. She noticed the strong scent of fumes seeping through the cracks of the door. Em, they think it was a suicide attempt. There were signs of carbon monoxide poisoning."

"Oh my God, no!" Emerlyn burst into tears, burying her head in her hands. "Dad, is he alive?"

"Yes, Em. He's in really bad shape, but there's a chance he'll pull through. But Em, there's more, honey."

Emerlyn's soul felt heavy and tired. She raised her bloodshot eyes from behind her cold hands and managed to mutter, "More?"

Her father put his hand on her shoulder and leaned in, "Em, it appears there really was a discharged firearm. It doesn't make much sense, but it seems Jack shot himself in the thigh just before passing out. Carbon monoxide poisoning is known to cause hallucinations, but the fact is we just don't have all the answers yet. By the time Jack's mother and father rushed him to the emergency room, he had almost bled out. It's a miracle they were able to stabilize him."

Chapter 6

Paige awoke to a cacophony of buzzing alarms on her phone, a screaming match happening just outside of her bedroom, and a headache from Hell.

"Another stress headache," Paige groaned as she turned over in bed. "Looks like I won't be posting a new Halloween makeup tutorial on Youtube today. I guess a little civility is too much to ask of my parents. Maybe I could just post a compilation video of their arguments. I could call it, 'Highlight Reel of Horror'. Yea, that has a nice ring to it. They'd probably find a way to sabotage that, too."

Sadly, verbal abuse had become sort of a morning routine for her family, thus the expectation of stress and headaches. Paige's parents were only happy with each other when they were drunk, busy being the center of attention, or both. She could only assume that this particular argument was about some aspect of their stupid Halloween Ball. She was counting down the hours until her parents tried to prop her up like some sort of a cheap whore. It was humiliating. Paige was tired of old, rich, intoxicated politicians gawking at her body and making lewd comments under their breath. They never even attempted to hide their insatiable thirst for youth. What they wanted was obvious, and it was repulsive.

Paige squinted her eyes at the screen of the humming phone. She fully expected to see Jack's contact photo appear with at least half a dozen missed calls next to his name, but there were none from him. He hadn't even bothered to send a single text; then again, neither had she. A deep swell of sadness quickly infected the pit of her stomach. It was a chasmic, nauseating heaviness, the kind that usually hits you near the end of a deteriorating relationship. Paige tried her best to bury those kinds of thoughts, but lately their demise seemed inevitable. Her parents despised him, and he despised her parents. Who could blame him? They were terrible people. None of it was Jack's fault, but the push and pull of it was becoming exhausting.

"Mr. C.?" Paige murmured to herself as she thumbed through the log of missed calls. "He left a voicemail…" Her heart sank. Jack's father only made important calls. He hated cellphones. He and Thomas had long, late night conversations about the effects of 5G radiation on the human body; and they were convinced that it would enslave us, induce a sort of psychomotor retardation, or slowly kill us all. Paige's wide eyes watered with fear as she reluctantly clicked on the voice message.

Sick with guilt-induced biliousness, Paige continued to replay Mr. C.'s voicemail in her head while fighting back the sudden urge to vomit. She traced the outline of the hospital room numbers with her fingertips, straining to see through her tears; and her thoughts skipped like a broken record as she quietly approached Jack's bedside.

"We'll give you a few minutes," Mr. C. said as he and his wife sullenly exited the room.

It was quiet, and the air was sterile. For a moment, Paige's mind was lost in an ocean of silence; but her wandering thoughts were quickly interrupted by the beeping of the Vital Signs Monitor that stood next to Jack's bed. As she stepped forward and placed her hand on his head, her eyes flooded with tears and her heart drowned in a vat of guilt.

"Life's not fair," Paige whispered as she gently ran her fingers through his thick, dark hair. "I'm so sorry for the way we left things last night. I know you were trying to be adventurous for me. You always put in the extra effort on Halloween; I was just so scared, Jack. When I saw the image of that dead woman between us, I felt like my mind broke. My world was already so shattered; it's been that way for a while now. I was scared and confused long before we ever stepped foot into the hollow. I have these dreams of leaving this place and escaping the suffocating hold that my parents have over me." Paige looked up at the ceiling as though she were half-confessing her troubles to some higher entity. "I know that you can feel our love growing thin, Jack. I can see it in your eyes. You hide the pain well behind that charming smile of yours, but I can see it. It's not fair to you, and it's never gonna be. I have no choice but to leave, and I know you won't come with me. I just never imagined this is how we'd spend our last Halloween together." Paige slowly closed her teary eyes; vivid, sentimental memories flickered through her mind. "I've brought a lot of emotional baggage into this relationship, and you've been so good to me," Paige's chin trembled as she struggled to hold back another wave of saline tears. "Oh, God, Jack. Please tell me you're not in this hospital because of me. I can't lose you, not like this." Paige began to weep uncontrollably as she laid her head at his bedside. "I'm still in love with you, Jack. I need you to know that."

Inchmeal, Emerlyn and Thomas opened the door while Max anxiously lingered in the hallway with Jack's mother and father.

"Paige, is it okay if we come in? Are you alright?" Emerlyn inquired with the gentlest of tones.

Without looking back at the door, Paige continued to sob, and Emerlyn instinctively rushed over to her side and cradled her with hugs. Thomas's glasses began to fog as he, too, wept for Jack. He and Max made their way to Jack's bedside, saddened and confused by the whole situation. In the back of their minds, they secretly wondered if all of this was somehow related to Amelia, Reverend Holcomb, or that missing grimoire.

Thomas's thoughts raced as he attempted to objectively analyze the situation. Jack is clearly not suicidal, and if he were, surely he would have chosen a different method to take his own life. Right? He reasoned quietly in his own mind. I heard Mr. C. talking to Max about possible hallucinations from the carbon dioxide, but why was he in that truck? It just doesn't add up.

"Thomas? Are you talking to yourself again?" Max asked in a concerned voice. "I can see your lips twitching and shit. It's kinda creeping me out, Dude." Thomas's eyes stared into some unknown dimension while he played out a plethora of scenarios in his head.

"Thomas!" Emerlyn quietly commanded. "What's going on inside that head of yours?"

Thomas blinked his eyes and awkwardly snapped back to reality. "Sorry, Em. We need to talk, but this isn't the right time or place," he replied gently.

Paige lifted her head from Jack's side and looked across the bed at Thomas. "What is it?"

The four quietly exited the room and made their way to an empty lounge area. Thomas closed the door and the girls sat down on the couch while Max fumbled around with the vending machine.

"Hey, Bro, Mom's debit card isn't working with this dumb machine," Max complained as he continued to drive his finger into the keypad menu. "I totes need a protein shake. You got any change? I'm famished," he continued, placing the back of his hand on his forehead for dramatic punctuation.

"Just sit down, Max. We'll snack after the recapitulation," Thomas snapped at his brother.

"The re-capit-ya-what?" Max asked in a sarcastically confused manner.

"The recap, Max. Sit down for the fuckin' recap," Thomas answered in his usual annoyed tone. As Max and Thomas sat down, they began to nervously fidget on the couch across from the girls.

Paige leaned forward, squinting at Thomas. "Well, spit it out. What's on your mind? What exactly are we recapitulating?"

"There's a lot on my mind," Thomas replied, "but there are too many unknown variables right now. For starters, I don't think there's a single person in this room who thinks Jack would actually try to commit suicide."

Emerlyn's left eye twitched as she quietly struggled to keep thoughts of her grandmother and that room out of her mind.

Paige's eyes began to tear and her voice cracked. "Jack and I had a really bad fight last night. That thing on his phone, the reverend guy's grave, the feeling of being followed, all of it… It was just too much. I could tell that he wanted to apologize, but I wouldn't let him. I just kept yelling at him, and then I just left him there, alone." Paige's chin began to tremble again. "Part of me thinks that he did this because of me."

Emerlyn leaned forward and put her arm around Paige. "This is not your doing. Do you understand?"

"Look guys there's more to Amelia's story than we've been told, and I think it might, somehow, have something to do with what happened to Jack. Just hear me out. Last night Max showed me something that he found in Reverend Holcomb's grave," Thomas said as he nervously shifted his eyes toward his brother, noticing a look of shame painted across his face.

"So Max robbed a grave?" Emerlyn asked in a monotone voice. "That's honestly not surprising," she continued, rolling her eyes in annoyance.

"Right now, that's besides the point," Thomas answered. "It was a book, Holcomb's personal Bible. In it, he had a series of short inscriptions, most of them irrelevant to our encounters last night. However, there was a particular entry that mentioned Amelia Groeh."

The girls flinched at the name, and the energy of the room shifted. "What did it say?" Paige asked as she and Emerlyn both sat on the edge of their seats.

"I have the book in mom's car outside. You can read it for yourselves if you'd like. In summary, it seems to suggest that Amelia might have actually been involved in witchcraft. At the very least, someone in the surrounding community was a practitioner of a grimoire."

"It's a book of spells," Max interjected.

Thomas glanced over at his brother and then continued. "At the end of the entry, Reverend Holcomb expresses confusion, doubt, and regret." Thomas rubbed his forehead and adjusted his glasses. "Here's what we can infer from Holcomb's inscription: a grimoire was recovered, Amelia was accused and executed by the townspeople for being a practitioner of the book, and both the book and Amelia were buried somewhere together. My guess is near the tree where she was hanged. Then, Amelia's body and the grimoire just vanished. It is also worth mentioning that the reverend fell sick with what he called the affliction, and he most likely died shortly after Amelia's execution."

"Thomas, not to sound unimpressed by your findings, but what does any of this have to do with Jack?" Emerlyn asked, the haunting tone of worry in her voice.

"Em, I don't know exactly, but it all seems to be connected. When did things really start to get weird for us? I bet you're thinking it was when I fell into the grave or when we saw the woman in that photo, right? Wrong."

"Fake news!" Max interjected, again. "Wrong!"

Thomas rolled his eyes and continued, "It was almost immediately after Mr. C. told us the legend of Amelia. As soon as we started looking for her, we felt like we were being followed, Em began seeing apparitions, and everyone had a general sense of uneasiness."

Thomas looked around the lounge at the various vintage pumpkin and ghost decorations on the walls, then looked back at the girls. "We live for this season. Every one of us loves Halloween, haunted houses, and horror movies, including Jack. This is the first time that we've been genuinely terrified of a little ghost story. Then, there's that church, the creepy tree, and obviously the photograph on Jack's phone... I hate to say it, but I think we might have stirred some sort of a demonic hornet's nest. Look, I don't have all the answers yet, but it's possible that we've been cursed. What happened with Jack could just be the beginning. I think we need to go back to the hollow and, at the very least, put this Bible back where it belongs. The only way we can combat any of this is to try and understand it."

A dead silence filled the room as they attempted to fully comprehend the severity of the situation. Suddenly, a familiar sound resonated from inside the lounge. Creak. Crack. Emerlyn's eyes widened, and the hairs on the back of her neck stood up. Thoughts of her grandmother's rocking chair and that dismal, dark room quickly suffused her mind. Before she could say anything, there was a loud BANG. Emerlyn, Paige, and Thomas all gasped while frantically surveying the room. In juxtaposition, Max calmly stood up and walked over to the vending machine out of curiosity.

"Sweet! My protein shake finally vended! I'm starving," Max exclaimed as he began to noisily rip the plastic banding from the bottle. "You know, I know this whole situation is super terrifying and stuff; but the whole time Thomas was talking about ghosts and curses, all I could think about was this delicious drink. Now I have it, so you have my full attention. Scout's honor."

Paige took a moment to catch her breath while scowling at Max. She secretly envied his innocence and the way he seemed completely oblivious to the seriousness of their bizarre predicament. She thought hard but couldn't remember a time where she ever felt that sense of sinlessness for herself.

"Look, there's nothing in this world that I want more than to help you fix the fucking train wreck of a night that we had, but I can't just leave Jack. He hasn't woken up since last night." Her tired, red eyes started to fill up with tears, again. "If he wakes up... I mean, when he wakes up, I need to be here for him. It's bad enough that my parents are only lending me the SUV as a way of bribing me to make an appearance at that stupid party tonight." Paige sighed and attempted to swallow the lump of guilt that seemed to be forever lodged in her airway. "My hands are tied guys. I'm sorry. I really am, but this is where I need to be."

"Say no more, Paige." Emerlyn placed her hand on the back of Paige's head and cleared her throat in an effort to conceal the sound of sorrow in her voice. "Thomas, if you believe there's a chance that this is all connected, if you say we need to go back to that hollow, then I believe you." Emerlyn's deep blue eyes seemed to unintentionally burn a hole right through Thomas's soul as she confidently stared back at him, forcing a half-grin upon her face. "Paige, your place is here with Jack. We know that, and we know that he needs you. I'll go with the guys. We're going to figure this out. I promise."

Since her grandmother's death, Emerlyn's father had been a source of strength and the voice of reason inside of her head. Now, Emerlyn felt like it was her turn to be strong for her friends; she couldn't help but hear the sound of her father's dejection embedded deep within her own voice.

"Then, it's settled," Thomas replied as he looked back at Emerlyn. "Holcomb's Bible is still in the dash of Mom's car, so I'll drive. We better get going. The hollow is pretty far from here."

Max scoffed, "Mom sleeps all day, anyway. Probably won't even notice we're gone."

Chapter 7

Max crawled into the backseat of the car, and Emerlyn sat up front. Thomas leaned towards her to open up the dashboard, revealing the crinkled leather of Holcomb's Bible. The energy inside the car was heavy, but part of Thomas still wanted to lean just a little bit closer to Emerlyn and kiss her on the cheek. He took a deep breath and exhaled slowly in an effort to focus on the matter at hand.

"So, what's the game plan?" Emerlyn asked as she carefully thumbed through the book. Her eyes watered at the very sight of the reverend's handwriting. She could almost feel his voice rumble through her chest as she traced the curve of every letter with her eyes, mouthing the words under her breath.

Thomas's grip on the steering wheel tightened, and a bit of panic began to rumble in the pit of his gut. The truth was that he didn't really have much of a plan, only questions that needed answers. He hadn't realized it before, but people were depending on him to find those answers.

"Well, we definitely need to get that Bible back to its rightful owner. I think we've extracted all the information that we need from it," he answered nervously. "Having a dead man's holy book might not qualify as cause for a curse, but it's definitely not positive karma. Maybe we can have a look around? I was thinking about the apparitions you've been seeing. Could you tell me a little more about them?" Thomas asked, glancing over at Emerlyn.

"Thomas, I need to tell you something," Emerlyn answered abruptly. "I think I saw someone in my grandmother's room this morning." Her voice trembled as she spoke.

"Em, what? No one goes in that room! What were you doing in there?" Thomas pleaded. He could see Max's eyes widen in the rearview mirror.

"I heard noises. I didn't want to go in that room! You know I didn't!" Emerlyn began to quietly sniffle as she looked out the passenger window, avoiding eye contact. "Someone was sitting in her rocking chair, Thomas. At first, I thought I was dreaming, but I didn't get a wink of sleep. It felt like someone started walking towards me. No matter how hard I tried, I couldn't see them." Emerlyn rubbed her eyes and turned to Thomas. "My dad found me in the room and pulled me into the hallway. I swear, I thought it was all just a dream. Then, my parents told me about Jack, and it turned into a fucking nightmare! Part of me wonders if I'm still asleep. I can't stop thinking about that damn photo on Jack's phone, and I keep seeing some sort of specter. Am I going crazy, Thomas?" Her eyes begged for an answer that would somehow bring her peace.

"No, Em. You're not crazy," Thomas answered. "I don't think it's a coincidence that you were visited by someone or something from the other side just moments before you found out about Jack."

"The other side?" Max asked, leaning forward in his seat.

"The other side of the veil," Thomas paused as he slowly collected his thoughts like tiny pieces of a puzzle. "It's like a barrier that separates the living from the dead. Most cultures believe that this invisible barrier is thinnest on Halloween." Thomas stopped the car and placed it in park. "Speaking of barriers…"

"Build the wall!" Max shouted. "Make America great again!"

"Shut up, Max!" Thomas retorted. He longed for a day in the not-so-distant future when no one would understand Max's current events jokes. "We're back at the trailhead, and it's all on foot from here. Oh, and don't forget the Bible, Max."

"At least this time, we can see where we're going!" Max facetiously replied as he clumsily exited the car.

"Just because the sun's out, doesn't mean it's safe," Emerlyn quickly interjected. "Anything could be in this thicket, including wild animals."

"Tell me about it," Thomas chimed in. "There are so many variables at play. Have you guys ever seen Dave Wascavage's *Suburban Sasquatch*?"

"No! Tell me what that is," Max implored.

Emerlyn giggled in the background, "Glad to see you haven't lost your sense of humor, Thomas."

"Humor? That movie is absolutely terrifying." Thomas grinned as he turned to his brother. "I'll show it to you when we get back home, Max."

The trio started down the trail and into the woods. Thomas took note of the dried up riverbeds that ran underneath the thick canopy of the forest. He hadn't noticed it in the dark of night, but the winding path that led to the meadow was no path at all. It was once a small runoff that branched into two directions.

"So we went left last night. Right, guys?" Thomas's tone of uncertainty, begging for reassurance.

"First you say left. Then you say right. Which is it? You're confusing," Max joked.

"Ha, ha, ha. So funny, Max," Thomas replied.

"Has to be left. I can still sort of see our footprints," Emerlyn answered as she examined disturbances in the red dirt. "The other trail is barely visible. There's no way we would've seen it in the dark."

"Well, we know what awaits us on the left-hand path. Should we check out the other trail for a ways?" Thomas asked as he stared further into the hollow and adjusted his glasses.

"The visitant that I saw last night--" Emerlyn paused mid-thought, and a cool, gentle breeze began to shuffle the leaves on the ground. "It seemed to be lingering on that side of the clearing. Maybe it was trying to show me something," she answered in a deep, serious tone. "I feel pulled to it, like, we have to check it out."

"Agreed," Thomas answered. "We're here to find answers."

"And to put this book back! Don't forget about that!" Max interjected.

"Don't worry Max. We won't be long," Thomas assured his brother. "We'll follow it for a bit. If we don't see anything of interest, we'll turn back."

As the three pushed further down the narrowing creek bottom, they noticed remnants of past settlements littered across the forest floor. Rusted steel rings from wagon wheels, cast iron cooking equipment, and old plow parts were among the scattered pieces.

"Someone definitely lived out here," Emerlyn muttered under her breath as she stooped down to examine an oxidized pot. She ran her fingertips across the marred metal surface, and the energy in the air shifted.

There was an unhurried chill crawling across her skin and nipping at her earlobes.

"Where the fuck is Max? Please, tell me you know where he is," Thomas exhorted.

"I don't know. I'm sorry, Thomas. I was. . .distracted. He couldn't have gone far," Emerlyn responded nervously.

"Hey! Over here!"

Thomas and Emerlyn heard Max's voice just up the trail. They looked at each other and ran toward the sound.

"Come quick! I found something," Max yelled.

As the two caught up to Max, they fought to catch their breath. "Didn't you learn anything from last night? I fell into a grave, Max! Bad things can happen out here," Thomas scolded as he gasped for air. "What? No smartass comeback this time? Let me borrow your asthma inhaler, Dweeb." Thomas remained hunched over, trying to slow his breathing.

"Thomas, look," Emerlyn urged as she pointed to the menacing, dark outline of a house in shambles. It was tucked away, deep within the shadows of the hollow. Time had not been kind to the little cabin, but it appeared to be mostly intact. It still had some of its old, wavy glass windows from pioneer times. The roof was missing small sections, but the walls were still sturdy and standing.

Thomas put his hand on his brother's shoulder and looked at Emerlyn as he continued to catch his breath. "Do you think it's… I mean, could it be hers?" Thomas stuttered.

Max began to tremble as Thomas gently tugged on his shoulder, pulling him away from the shanty. Emerlyn took a step towards the tenebrous ruins of the porch.

"Wait," Thomas whispered. "We'll go together." Emerlyn turned to face the boys and nodded in agreement.

As the three slowly approached the dilapidated dwelling, they cautiously peered through the mildew-stained windows. Tiny beams of light bled through various holes in the rickety roof and spilled onto the grimy, dust-covered floorboards. In a ceremonious fashion, Thomas, Emerlyn, and Max placed their trembling hands on the front door and began to count aloud.

"One, two, three!" They pushed the old, wooden door.

With a high-pitched squeal, it reluctantly opened, revealing a cloud of debris floating through faint bits of light. A swirl of wind carried orange and yellow leaves into the cabin, and Emerlyn felt that old, familiar chill biting at the back of her neck.

The dust settled, and Thomas began to observe the contents of the room. A small fireplace caked with sable soot was built into the right wall. It contained a black iron pot similar to the ones found near the property. A series of shelves with various little glass bottles and fountain pens lined the wall at the 1 o'clock position, and a doorway to a corridor lay directly ahead. Emerlyn and Max looked to the left of the room and noticed another mildewy window that was riddled with tiny cracks. The rest of the room was barren, lacking any furniture or other accoutrements. Max took a knee and carefully wiped away the thick film of detritus that lined the splintered floorboards.

"Hey, guys. Check this shit out!" Max pointed to the boards leading into the hallway. Long scratch marks were carved deep into the wooden floor, seeming to continue out the door and onto the porch behind them. "Just like Mr. C. told us," Max muttered in disbelief. "She was dragged out of her own house." His eyes watered.

Thomas turned to his brother and pointed to the shelving near the hallway, "And the ink bottles are here, too." Thomas's thoughts were racing; the thud of his heart was almost jarring.

"That means her room should be just down the hall. According to the story, that's where they grabbed her." Emerlyn let out a slow, heavy exhale and nervously touched her crucifix necklace. "Shall we have a look?"

"Wait, I'm getting some serious *Evil Dead* vibes in here," Max cautioned. "I mean, I half-expected to see a '73 Oldsmobile parked out front. What if there's something waiting for us at the end of that hallway?"

"Well, I'm starting to think that's kind of the idea, Max," Thomas mumbled his reply. "We'll have to follow Em's lead on this one. She'll tell us if she sees anything."

Emerlyn stared intently as she started towards the dimly illuminated hall. The holes in the roof cast a haunting hue of apricot-colored light, and the intruding wind left a crisp chill in the air. With every step, the floorboards creaked and cracked, making Emerlyn's skin crawl. She couldn't help but feel unsettled by the sound. As she passed through the doorway, Thomas reached forward and grabbed her hand. Max followed closely behind and tightly held his brother's sleeve. The three formed a chain, tiptoeing down the narrow corridor in unison.

The first room was on the right-hand side and had no door. Emerlyn peeked around the corner of the doorframe and peered into the ill-lit chamber. Her wide eyes struggled to make sense of the dark. She picked up her cellphone and used the display screen to illuminate the space. Inchmeal, Thomas and Max followed. She panned the phone from left to right, using it as a small floodlight. With every heavy thump of Emerlyn's heartbeat, her hand swayed, and the light capered through the shadows. There were no windows, closets, or furniture. It, too, was completely barren. A small section of the floor was missing from the corner, revealing dirt and rocks beneath the cabin. There was nothing of apparent interest, and the three let out a sigh of relief, quickly exiting the room.

The trio continued down the hall. Another empty chamber lied to the left of the corridor. They did a swift reconnaissance, again finding nothing of apparent interest. The floor was littered with pieces of the crumbling ceiling and rat droppings. A lone black widow weaved its tangled web of death around various insects that had fallen victim to the allure of its silky, electrostatic threads.

"God, I hate spiders," Thomas grumbled.

For Thomas, the shimmering, crimson hourglass tattooed on the spider's ebony abdomen was nature's cruel reminder that time was running out for everyone. In the same way in which the arachnid's web summoned insects to the slaughter, so, too, had a shadowy apparition and this cabin called unto them. The fear of death festered in everyone's mind, and the howling wind whipped through the holes in the hallway, whistling like a wild wendigo wraith. That eerie sound left Emerlyn's skin riddled with goosebumps.

"Only one more room to go," Thomas whispered with a heavy lump in his throat.

The closer they got to the bedroom, the faster and louder his heart pounded in his chest. The air became still. The door was slightly ajar; and with the help of Max, he pushed it open the rest of the way. The creaking of the hinges was unnaturally loud in the unnerving silence that surrounded them. A dirty mirror still hung on the wall, further yellowed by age, with a small table and cracked basin directly beneath it. Thomas noted the remains of a broken bed frame in the far corner of the room.

"This was her room." Emerlyn's voice was barely above a whisper. She rubbed her arms in an effort to rid herself of the lingering goosebumps. She pointed to the floor. "Look." She stooped down, holding her cellphone light just above the splintered floorboards.

Thomas and Max turned their attention to the phone's anemic glow. Cavernous carvings from Amelia's nails bore through the wooden floor; a grossly discolored fingernail remained lodged inside one of the boards near the doorway. It reminded Thomas of what the inside of a coffin might look like during horrific cases of vivisepulture, victims scratching and clawing for dear life.

"She knew she was going to die." Thomas's words sounded even more introspective than usual.

"Maybe she knew long before the townspeople even grabbed her," Max replied, bemused by the troubling thought.

As he grew older, he found himself becoming more and more conspiratorial. He tried to conceal it by constantly cracking wise, but it was getting harder to hide. Perhaps, that's the sort of thing that happens when your brother watches *Leak Project* every night; all these years he thought it was bullshit. Max assumed Thomas was just a bit off his rocker; but now, in this moment, he was standing in the creepy bedroom of an alleged witch that was kidnapped, assaulted, and hanged by the neck until dead. Suddenly, all the ridiculous ramblings and conspiracy theories he'd heard about the Annunaki, secret societies, and otherworldly dimensions seemed all too real. Even the term conspiracy theorist was saturated in skepticism and doubt, since it's believed that it was coined by the CIA to discredit those who had the audacity to question an official narrative. And to top it all off, Max had a dead man's Bible in his back pocket with a handwritten account referencing the mysterious disappearance of a spellbook and the deceased witch's body.

"If she really knew the mob was going to come for her that night, she must have left some sort of a clue or message behind for a relative or a friend to find." Thomas grabbed his cellphone out of his pocket and proceeded to use it as a flashlight. "Look for symbols, words, or anything that looks out of the ordinary," Thomas instructed as he used the dim light to examine the underside of the small table set beneath the mirror.

Leadership was not his strong suit. Normally, Jack would do this sort of thing, and Thomas still felt very conflicted about being back in the hollow. Part of him just wanted to put the Bible back and run home, but he could also feel Emerlyn's need to be here. Lately, she'd seen things that no one else could see, and it terrified him.

Max followed his brother's lead and took a knee beside the broken bed frame, tediously examining it for any unusual markings. "Nothing here, Broseph."

Emerlyn stood by Thomas, gently prying the old mirror from the wall. "I was so sure I'd find something, but I've got nothing here either," she added.

"Same here," Thomas replied. His brow wrinkled with confusion as he adjusted his glasses. "There's something here. I can feel it."

"Me too," Emerlyn replied. She noticed the unmistakable outline of a towering, dark figure standing at the opposite end of the hallway, slowly waving. "Or more like someone here."

Admittedly, it wasn't the only phantom she'd encountered; but this was very different. It was the first full-bodied apparition she'd seen so clearly, and it stood several feet taller than any man. Though the terribly prodigious phantasm manifested in the darkest of shadows, it was overwhelmingly darker, heavier in nature. She blinked several times, hoping it was just a simple case of shadow matrixing; but the waving silhouette remained, almost playful in appearance. There was a cold quiver in her voice. "I see someone in the front room." Emerlyn's voice cracked. As she spoke, the phantom dissipated, leaving behind a black plasmic haze near the entrance of the cabin.

Max poked his head into the hallway, "I don't see anything, Em."

"Trust me. Someone or something is in there," she replied, her voice unnaturally shaky.

"We trust you, Em," Thomas reassured her as he placed his trembling fingers on her shoulder. "I'm betting if we're going to find anything, it'll probably be in there."

Emerlyn nodded, and the three cautiously headed back towards the entrance.

"Max and I can sift through the ash and examine the stones in the fireplace for any symbols or hidden flues. It's a longshot, but there might be something in there," Thomas said.

Emerlyn motioned toward the filth-stained bottles and rusted pens on the shelves. "I'll try over there."

A faint fog still lingered in the room, and its murk collected around the base of the splintered shelving. She secretly wondered if the boys could see it, too.

She brushed away the tangled cobwebs from the grimy glass, picked up one of the bottles, and wiped it off with her sleeve. Emerlyn took a moment to look around the room. Standing amidst the ghostly mist, she could easily imagine Amelia bustling around the kitchen, her long skirts brushing against the floorboards while she busied herself with cooking. In her mind's eye, she saw her seated at the table by candlelight, the quill of her pen scratching across the paper as she wrote. Emerlyn shook her head to clear it; she replaced the bottle and continued to search the shelves. On the bottom shelf, Emerlyn found a simple, plain rectangular box.

"Ugh, Thomas..." Max's hands began to shake as he pointed his light up the chimney. "I see something looking at me."

"What do you mean looking at you?" Thomas asked, the urgency in his voice commanded an immediate response.

"I see eyes! Thomas, I fucking see eyes!" Max quickly backed out of the chimney, a trail of black dust followed him.

"Are you serious?" Thomas asked as he bent down on one knee and slowly inched his light into the fireplace. He reluctantly peeked into the chimney. "Max, I see them too! They're coming closer..." Thomas's voice trailed off as he stared through the swirling soot into two amber irides that quickly began to look more like glowing pools of golden honey.

Emerlyn turned from the shelving, "I hear something."

"I hear it, too," Max whispered.

"Thomas, what do you see? Thomas?" Emerlyn supplicated, but there was no response.

A charcoal-colored mass was attached to the approaching amber orbs. Thomas was frozen with fear as the two eyes multiplied into dozens more, twitching and moving about. Suddenly, the fireplace came alive. A cacophony of high-pitched squeaks, pitter-pattering flutters, and jarring discordance filled the room, overloading Thomas's senses. Dozens of black masses surged towards his face as he fell backwards, sending him sprawling across the floor. A series of erratic, fitful shadows followed close behind, bolting and wavering across the grotty room.

"Desmodontinae! Vampire bats!" Thomas yelled as he covered his face, rolling across the filthy floor.

Another swirl of leaves twisted through the open door, causing even more chaos inside the cabin. Emerlyn instinctively took shelter under one of the sullied shelves, shielding her face and screaming in terror.

"I don't want coronavirus!" Max caterwauled.

The feeling of fluttering wings against his scalp sent a frisson down Max's back, triggering his fight-or-flight mechanism. Unfortunately, as he flailed and scuttled out of the frightful shanty, most of the crepuscular creatures flittered just behind him. He took an impromptu nosedive off of the porch, and the fidgety vampires scattered across the rocky ravine. Max exhaled in pain as he rolled onto his back. Emerlyn continued to scream bloody murder inside the cabin as Thomas struggled to remove a stray bat tangled in her hair.

Small fissures in the ceiling continued to breathe, and another violent draft spiraled through the corridor, causing the cabin door to slam shut. Thomas and Emerlyn darted through the darkness, pulling on the door handle with all their might.

"Max, help! We're locked inside!" Thomas yelled to his brother.

Max rushed to the porch. With as much power and speed as he could muster, he rammed his shoulder into the door; but it did not budge. Frustrated and desperate, he attempted to kick it down to no avail.

"Thomas, I'm sorry. I can't get it open!" Max yelled as he pounded his fists on the boards.

"Em, we can go down the hall and crawl through the hole in the floor!" Thomas exclaimed as his mind searched for a feasible escape route.

"Fuck it! I'm done with this place!" Emerlyn shined her light towards the shelving near the hallway. "All we need is this," she said as she grabbed the wooden box on the bottom shelf.

"Em, what are you…?"

Before Thomas could finish his question, Emerlyn hurriedly waltzed over to the mildewy window at the far end of the room and launched the small box straight through the wavy glass. Thomas rushed over to remove the remaining shards from the windowpane. Max ran around the side of the house, helping Emerlyn and Thomas make a swift exit. The three backed away from the eerie cabin and giggled hysterically.

"What a fuckin shit show," Thomas removed his glasses and rubbed his eyes in disbelief.

"I didn't know you had it in you, Em," Max joked as the paradoxical laughter subsided. "That's one hell of an arm you've got there."

"There's a lot you don't know about me." Emerlyn smiled as her attention drifted.

She walked over to the open box she'd used to breach the window. The inside was empty; but when she shook it, she heard a rustling sound. It was so faint that Emerlyn wondered if she'd actually heard it at all. Maybe she imagined it simply because she wanted to find something. She tilted the box from side-to-side and noticed a slight gap along one of the edges. She pressed the corner, and the bottom of the box flipped up revealing a hidden compartment.

"Em, how did you know?" Thomas curiously inquired.

Ignoring Thomas's inquiry, Emerlyn reached inside the secret compartment and removed a single, terribly defaced sheet of paper. "Thomas, have a look at this." Emerlyn's eyes widened with fear and disbelief.

The texture and weight of the page in her hands felt less like traditional paper and more like crumpled leather. Deep wrinkles plagued its surface, the blackened edges appeared to be burned, and the crimson ink seemed to bleed from the folio, right before their eyes. The document was double-sided, and it appeared as though it had been crudely ripped right from a fan-made, Lovecraftian collection. Foreign languages, symbols, and letters were inscribed front and back amidst several grotesque illustrations of dead human beings, demonic entities, and various methods of suicide. The page was very old and had been translated several times over. The most recent of which was a series of English translations. Aggressively carved, handwritten warnings and foul language were superimposed beneath the blood-red illustrations.

Max inched his way closer to Emerlyn and Thomas. Holding his side, he walked with a slight stagger that he'd incurred from his recent injuries.

His voice cracked as he read from the front of the page, "A live burial must be performed on the possessed before it's too late." Above the scribbled words was a detailed illustration of a mangled, mutilated body clawing at the edges of a burial pit. "When the veil is thin, the suicide dybbuk can be released from its tomb." Max's skin crawled as he recalled the opening of Holcomb's grave followed by Jack's strange, apparent suicide attempt.

"A demon sleeps beneath the bleeding tree," Thomas whispered the words written beneath graphic depictions of a demon performing heinous sexual acts on men, women, and children. "Each life taken in the night is another slave to the hive. The Dream Demon will rot your fucking soul!"

Emerlyn turned over the page. An elaborate, blood-red drawing of a book with a grotesque appearance was set inside an upside down pentagram, a perversion of the pagan pentacle of protection. Each point of the star held a decaying, decrepit face for a total of five decomposing craniums. A sixth, inhuman face, was stitched across the cover of the book that lay in the center of the star.

"My name is Amelia Groeh. I took this page from a grimoire hidden beneath the church. Holcomb will likely come for me." Emerlyn took a deep breath and looked at Thomas. "Amelia," her eyes teared up as she continued to read from the document. "I don't think he knows it, but there are other, more generous patrons in his flock who possess pages from the book." Beneath the ink of her words was an older series of small sketches depicting various methods of suicide accompanied by short descriptions. "Truncatione, strangulavit, sahaq, venenum, carnificare, naze al' ahsha'. " Emerlyn struggled and stuttered through the ancient ink of Latin and Arabic words. Though she was literate in neither language, the overly graphic drawings told her all she needed to know. "Mutilation, strangulation, crushed to death, poisoned, decapitation, and disembowelment."

"Parasomnia pseudo-suicide," Thomas mumbled more words from the page. He looked up at Max and Emerlyn. "Sleepwalker's suicide and a Dream Demon. . .These suicides from Amelia's story were caused by some sort of a parasitic entity. It appears to kill you in your sleep."

"Is that what almost happened to Jack?" Max asked, a deep sense of dread attached to the tone of his voice. "Did it trick Jack into hurting himself because he released the demon?"

"Released the demon? What are you talking about, Max?" Thomas asked.

"After your leg got caught inside of Holcomb's coffin, Jack had to pry it open. Remember?" Max's words were breathy as panic still swelled in his chest. "You said it yourself. The whole thing about the veil being thinnest around Halloween, you know? Well, this page says the same thing! And we were all there. It's probably coming for us, too!"

"Why would the dybbuk be trapped inside Holcomb's coffin?" Emerlyn's eyes shifted from Max to Thomas.

Thomas adjusted his glasses, "Well it wouldn't unless…"

"Unless Holcomb was buried alive while under its influence," Emerlyn interrupted.

"Max let me see that Bible again." Thomas pointed to his brother's back pocket.

"Gladly!"

Thomas quickly flipped through the pages, turning to Holcomb's last note once more. "My attempts however, did not satiate the Devil's hunger. Death is upon me. The tomb was disturbed and the spellbook is missing. As I feel the affliction taking over, I am left to wonder whether or not I am the foolish sinner who lent his hand in the execution of an innocent girl in the name of false accusations. Or has Amelia Groeh truly transcended Death and risen from the very grave that I dug with my own two hands? God, deliver us from Evil."

"Holcomb knew he was going to die by the hands of the Devil," Emerlyn added. "He referred to it as the affliction. The question is whether or not he was actually buried alive."

"And whether he was a willing participant of the burial or just another unwilling sacrifice," Thomas closed the Bible and looked up at his brother. "I think it's time we put this thing back where it belongs. I need to examine that coffin. And just for the record Max, everyone knows COVID-19 is a bioweapon. The bats didn't give you coronavirus."

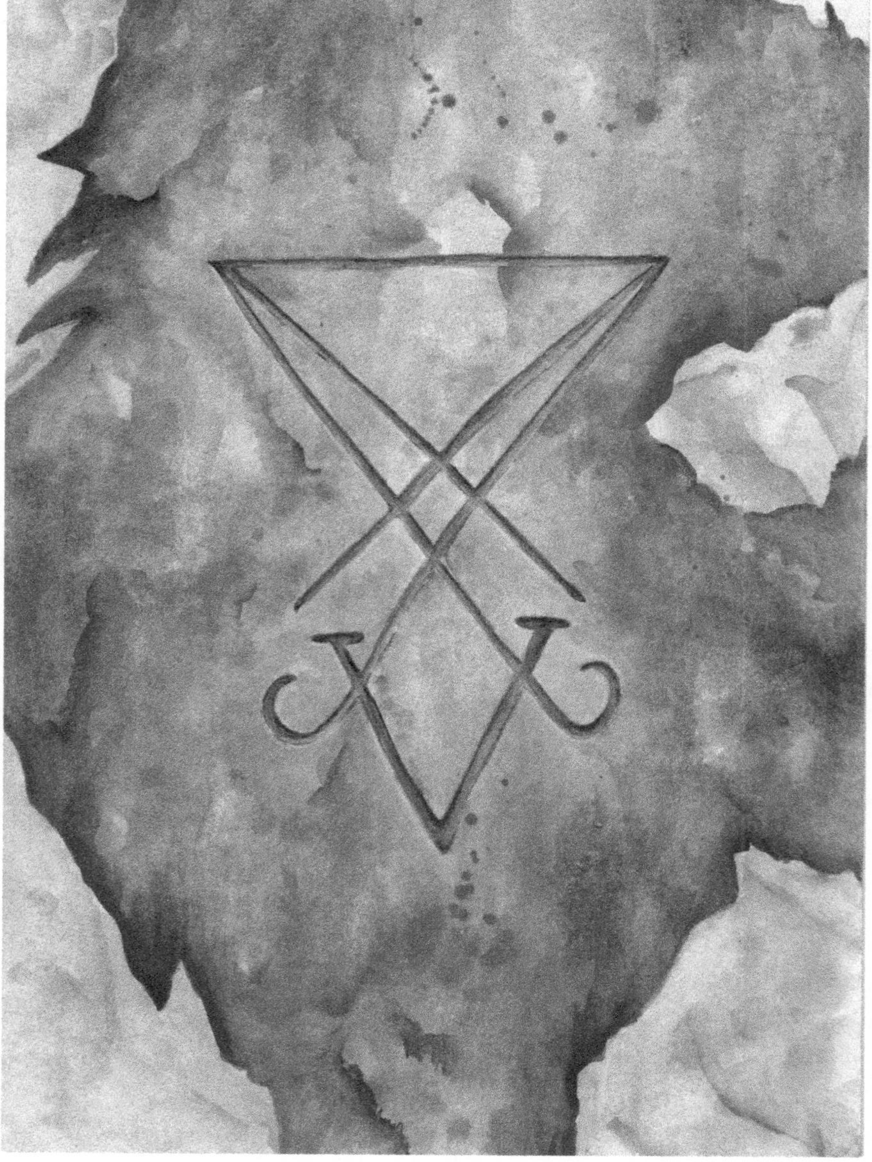

Chapter 8

There was a light tapping on the door. "Mr. and Mrs. Carter, I'd like to ask you a few questions about your son," a local deputy asked as he slowly entered the room.

"Yes, of course," Mr. C. replied.

"Paige, would you mind giving us the room for a few minutes?" Mrs. Carter asked, her tone soft and polite.

"Sure, no problem. I'll be in the lounge." Paige unsuccessfully attempted to wipe away the tears and the awful, tired look of grief she held upon her face. The skin on her cheeks felt raw, and her irritated eyes burned. "Do you need anything from the vending machine?"

"No, I believe we're fine for now. Thanks," Mr. C. gestured toward the open door.

Paige nodded and managed to fake a slight grin of gratitude as she made eye contact with the investigating officer. It was about time someone finally showed up to figure this out. None of it made sense.

As Paige walked down the hall, she wondered if anyone had taken a look at Jack's phone. Most of his belongings were still at home. If the cops see a photo of a dead girl hanging from the tree behind us, will we be accused of murder? Or will it be chalked up to some disturbing Halloween decor? How deep will they dig into this incident? Paige thought to herself as her nervous heartbeat continued to race with no signs of slowing down. She could hear it pounding in the veins of her skull and secretly wondered if anyone else heard it, too. The very thought of being investigated for murder gave Paige a surge of anxiety; she quickly closed the door behind her as she retreated to the lounge. Paige knew she had to be careful with the conversations she had over the phone. She was well aware of the fact that a judge could issue a search warrant to sift through her phone records.

She stared down at her cellphone, contemplating whether or not she should text Emerlyn and the boys. They hadn't called or messaged, and it had been hours since they'd left the hospital. She was worried sick, or maybe she was just sick of being worried.

Paige looked over at the vending machine and managed to giggle as she thought about Max's obnoxious struggle to get a protein shake. The longing for that type of innocence still burned in the pit of her befouled spirit. It was lunchtime, but her stomach still felt too nauseated to eat. Paige walked into the women's bathroom, locked the door, and stared at her reflection through the smudges in the mirror. She'd always been the vain one of the group, having to keep up appearances for the sake of her parents' social status.

"Look at me now, Mom." Paige mumbled under her breath as she examined the deep wrinkles of sleep deprivation and emotional trauma carved into her skin.

She hadn't had much rest lately. There was so much more going on than Jack's incident. So many secrets to keep and so much pressure to be perfect. Paige reached into her purse to retrieve her makeup, accidentally spilling it into the sink. "Fuck! Fuck! Fuck!" she exclaimed, frantically scrambling to put the contents of her purse back in their proper places.

She froze and stared at the last item lying near the drain. It was pointless to check again, she thought. In truth, Paige couldn't blame her nausea on Jack's hospitalization or recent emotional turmoil. Morning sickness had plagued her for the past several days, and the test results were always the same. She grabbed the pregnancy test out of the sink and fell to her knees, sobbing on the filthy floor.

"God, tell me what to do. How could I ever be a good mother?" Paige's voice quavered as she looked up at the blinding, white lights on the blemished bathroom ceiling, her burning tears blurring her vision. "Jack cannot leave this world. Not yet! He doesn't even know he's going to be a father! He deserves to know! Goddammit!" Paige took a deep breath and exhaled slowly. "I need him. We need him," she mumbled as she looked down, placing her trembling hands on her tiny belly.

There was a light tapping on the bathroom door. "Paige, are you in there?" Mrs. Carter asked.

"Yes. Just a minute, please." Paige's voice calmly reverberated in stark contrast to the shaking girl in the bedaubed mirror.

"Paige, it's ok. Take your time. I just wanted to let you know that Jack's father and I have to go back to the house for a few minutes. The police want to view our security footage from last night. It shouldn't take much longer than an hour or so..."

Paige felt another surge of sickness strike the pit of her gut. "Ugh... Oh-okay. Is there anything I can do to help?" Paige's mind raced as all her attention shifted to the thought of the grotesque photograph on Jack's phone. The police would never believe what really happened. Her only hope was that the cops would find what they were looking for on those security cameras. If that thing appeared on a shitty cellphone, it was bound to show up on expensive infrared cameras, right? Even as she contemplated the answer to her own question, Paige doubted herself.

"We were just hoping you could stay here with Jack until we are finished working with the investigators. We know your mother and father are expecting your attendance this evening. This shouldn't take very long. Is that okay, Paige?" Mrs. Carter asked, her soft voice slightly muffled by the door.

Paige slowly opened the bathroom, her face remarkably calm. "Yes, that'll be fine Mrs. C."

"Thank you, Paige. My son is very lucky to have you. We all are." Mrs. C. leaned forward and hugged Paige as they both cried softly.

As Paige walked back to Jack's room, her hands began to shake. She fidgeted with her phone, pretending to check non-existent social media messages and blank emails. It was some sort of a weird coping mechanism she'd developed in stressful situations. What she really wanted to do was contact Emerlyn and the boys, but she felt like she might be in the crosshairs of Big Brother. Thomas's government conspiracies always frightened Paige. She pretended that his long conversations with Mr. C. were ridiculous, but she'd seen too many of their theories play out in real life. Now, she wondered if she and her friends were actually being surveilled.

Paige put down her phone and sat next to Jack, holding his hand. He was still unconscious, but his mouth was mumbling something. "Jack! Can you hear me? Are you trying to talk to me, babe?"

Hearing the lonely sound of her own voice was enough to bring back the tears. Jack's mouth continued to maffle near inaudible syllables. Paige placed her ear to his lips in an effort to decrypt the hushed sounds, but it was just noise. It was all just noise.

"Wake up, Jack. Wake up for me," she whispered longingly into his ear. She stood up and carefully placed his hand on her belly. "There's someone I'd like you to meet, Jack."

Chapter 9

"If my limited experience as a boy scout has taught me anything, it's a strong sense of cardinal directions." Thomas thought out loud as he took one last look at Amelia's cabin. "We should be just east of Holcomb's grave. According to Mr. C's story, Amelia was dragged from this location to the tree. My guess is they used this overgrown wagon trail." Thomas pointed at a weathered path that started near the cabin. It went north and seemed to veer west, leading to the hollow.

"Ok, Bear Grylls. We get it," Max smirked. "Just don't lose the Bible along the way. I can't wait to get rid of that thing." Max's voice was sassy with a hint of seriousness.

"Should I leave the grimoire page here?" Emerlyn asked nervously as she stared at its horrific images.

"It's your call, Em. You found it," Thomas answered, uncertainty lingering in his voice.

"This isn't where the page belongs. I feel like we were meant to find it. I think we should bring it with us," Emerlyn replied. "What do you say, Max?"

"Don't look at me! I'm just a retired grave robber." Max held his hands in the air to reiterate his retirement.

"Okay, then. Sounds like it's settled. We better get moving," Thomas said as he started down the rock-strewn path. Emerlyn nodded and folded up the leathery paper before placing it in her pocket. Carrying such a burdensome artifact was no small thing, and the weight of its significance made her soul feel heavy and tired.

"Alright boys, let's get this crusade over with." Emerlyn managed to crack a smile as she instinctively reached for her crucifix. It was habitual, but comforting. After all, her life was beginning to feel like an episode of

The Paranormal Files. Demons, apparitions, witchcraft, what was next? She was questioning everything she'd ever known. Faith was her rock; and at the moment, it was all she had left. Well, faith and Thomas's lengthy text-rants about the validity of *SecureTeam10* videos. Maybe there really was so much more to life than Bible School had ever taught her.

"Help me understand," Emerlyn whispered as she looked towards the deep blue sky above.

"It's gonna be alright, Em," Max said as he put his arm around her shoulders.

"Well, what do ya know? I always knew you were a little sweetheart." Emerlyn grinned, poking fun at Max's genuine attempt at kindness.

"Don't get used to it," Thomas joked, turning to look back at his brother.

"Awe, come on! He's not that bad," Emerlyn replied with a wink.

Thomas stared intently. For the world, it was just a small, playful gesture. For Thomas, every curve and crease of her expression was an entire lexicon of emotion that burned beneath his chest. It was getting harder and harder to hide it.

"Alright, Romeo. Eyes up front. We need you focused! More *Man Vs Wild*. Less *Shakespeare in Love*," Max commanded, only half-jokingly.

"I don't dress like a fricken man, Max!" Emerlyn retorted.

Max had never bothered to watch romantic dramas. His poor reference made that pretty obvious.

Thomas snapped out of the love-induced daze. His face turned bright red as he adjusted his glasses. "I told ya not to get used to it, Em. I told ya!"

He couldn't help but giggle at the uncomfortable situation. He was more prepared to face down a literal demon than he was to tell Emerlyn how he really felt. Sure, it was probably obvious, but still…he never said the words. Emerlyn giggled and quickened her pace to catch up to Thomas, gently driving her elbow into his side to emphasize her good spirits. She hadn't noticed it until that moment, but she had grown awfully close to Thomas over the years.

"Almost there." Thomas pointed through the trees as the path curved towards the clearing. The old wagon trail cut straight through the tree line, passing near the gravesite. "There it is!"

"You sure you're not gonna fall in again, Bro?" Max snickered to mask his nervousness.

"You sure you're not gonna come out of retirement as a graverobber?" Emerlyn jokingly snapped back. "See? I have your back, Thomas."

"Thanks Em." Thomas managed to fake a quick smile; but his attention had drifted elsewhere.

Everything in the meadow looked so different during the daytime. There were other neglected gravestones near Holcomb's with simple engravings that indicated the former occupations of the dead. They had gone completely unnoticed under the cover of darkness, and the church was uncomfortably close by. Thomas's veins burned with fear just thinking about Amelia's words, knowing the evil grimoire probably still lay inside the undercroft of the church. Emerlyn and Max's silence indicated they, too, were feeling the fear.

Max peered over the side of Holcomb's grave; shards of the pine box were scattered along its edge. He looked to his brother. "Holy snappin' buttholes! Jack sure did a number on this coffin trying to get you out of here! I hope there's enough left for you to examine."

"There's enough," Thomas replied. He was literally seeing things in a new light. "It didn't make much sense last night. I couldn't understand how I could've fallen into a properly hollowed grave." Thomas walked around Holcomb's headstone and stooped down to examine the depth of the pit. "This grave is too shallow, which leads me to believe it was excavated in a hurry and without much care."

"Thomas, check this out." Emerlyn held up a lengthy portion of the broken coffin lid. "Scratch marks from the inside?"

"Vivisepulture..." The horrifying fingernail marks carved into the coffin lid looked exactly the way Thomas had imagined. He had accurately predicted the way the inside of the shivered casket would appear, but he was completely unprepared for the deep sense of disquietude that he felt seep down to the marrow of his bones. "So Holcomb was buried quickly because he was buried alive. Buried against his will but by whom?" Thomas swallowed the lump of angst that clung to the inside of his throat and continued to examine the inadequate pit.

"Someone who had knowledge of the page that Amelia took from the spellbook," Max replied.

Emerlyn felt her heart race from the thought of still having it in her pocket. Maybe it was just her imagination, but it felt like the evil within it might just burn a hole through her thigh.

"Are we thinking a former practitioner of the book? Or maybe just someone close to Holcomb who was studying it?" Emerlyn thought aloud as she placed her hand over her pocket. The page wasn't scorching her leg after all. She knew that, but she felt compelled to check.

Understandably, it gave off a weird energy. It wasn't necessarily completely wicked. It just was…it felt more like an ancient, verboten wisdom that predated the idea of good and evil. It may very well be the source of forbidden knowledge that Satan wished to bestow upon Adam and Eve. It was getting harder and harder to tell the difference between Lucifer and Prometheus. Why was the knowledge forbidden in the first place? Emerlyn couldn't help but wonder how the scripture of her religion must somehow intertwine with the ancient text she held in her pocket and the tale told by Mr. C. Hanging around Thomas always helped her see through the preachy bullshit; and she hoped that her spiritual presence benefitted his life, too. Even now, at the foot of a demonic burial site, she thought they made an excellent team, complimenting each other's strengths and weaknesses.

"Max, you do the honors," Thomas said as he handed over Holcomb's Holy Bible. "Do your best to put it back the way you found it. We have enough bad luck on our hands right now."

Max shuttered as he reluctantly grabbed the book from his brother. He carefully lifted the remains of Holcomb's right arm, sliding the book beneath it. The last thing he wanted was to accidentally break off this guy's arm. Max couldn't bear the thought of hearing Thomas screeching and scolding for the next twenty-four hours.

"There! It's done," Max declared.

"Did you put it back exactly how you found it?" Thomas interrogated his brother.

"Yea, Bro. I did." Max's eyes shifted from Thomas to the Bible under Holcomb's arm.

"Are you positive?" Thomas narrowed his eyes.

"Yea, basically. That's how I found it...Basically." Max began to second guess himself.

"Basically?" Emerlyn giggled. "Some graverobber you are."

"Grave robber. Not grave returner, Em-er-lyn," Max feistily retorted.

"We'll just leave well enough alone, I suppose," Thomas said as he respectfully replaced the broken pieces of the coffin, turning his attention to the church that ominously awaited down the wagon trail. Even in the light of day, it seemed more like a grotesque abattoir than a place of worship. "I know this goes without saying, but I really don't want to go back in there."

"Amelia said the book was once inside the church. Maybe the other graverobber mentioned in Holcomb's entry returned it there. We may already know how to stop the demon, but the options don't seem very practical or user friendly." Images of carnage from the page in Emerlyn's pocket flashed inside her head like a highlight reel of slaughtery and perturbation. "If we find the rest of the book, we might be able to learn more about this Dream Demon or where to find it. There may be a more permanent solution that doesn't require burying someone alive." Emerlyn exhaled slowly as she fought the fear that hid behind her trembling fingertips. "We don't even know if it's still attached to Jack or if it's just roaming around."

"How do we know it's not protecting the book?" Max asked. "For all we know, it could even be waiting inside the damn church!"

"We don't." Thomas started towards the decrepit temple. "We don't know much, but we know more than we did when we got here."

"Well, that's reassuring." Max turned to Emerlyn, wide-eyed and worried.

"It's gonna be alright, Max." Emerlyn put her arm around his shoulders and winked. Max knew she was just reciprocating his gesture of kindness, but it still brought him some comfort.

"That's some powerful wink you got there," Max grinned.

"Oh here we go again. Let's hear it, Max!" Thomas exclaimed in his signature I'm- annoyed-at-Max voice.

"What? I'm just saying…" Max pressed his lips together, stared at the ground, and focused on the crunching sound of the rocks beneath his feet in order to avoid laughing. Emerlyn, though in relatively good spirits, found herself avoiding the general direction of the tree. The church was scary enough, but that tree was horrifying. Everyone could feel it. With every reluctant step forward, the lurking shadow of the church drew nearer, the tangled web of branches above the sickly tree crept closer; and Thomas was reminded of the black widow inside Amelia's cabin that patiently awaited its prey.

Thomas stepped onto the raised platform, gazing up at the crumbling arch that was once a towering doorway to the church. The walls were in shambles, seemingly disintegrating before his eyes.

"I know this place is old; I just can't help but think that it was intentionally destroyed." He continued forward, surveying the temple while carefully traversing fragmented stones and splintered support beams that he'd seen the night before. Max and Emerlyn followed close behind.

As the three made their way deeper into the decrepit temple, a cawing murder of crows circled overhead, casting an array of wicked shadows that cavorted across the cluttered floor. The blinding midday sun punched through the partial roof, flooding the foundation in an ocean of burnt orange and lemony light.

"How very Edgar Allen Poe of you," Emerlyn muttered as she watched the noisy murder of crows fly over the grave plots and onto the tree where Amelia was hanged. She winced at the very sight of it, recalling the handwritten words from the page inside her pocket: A demon sleeps beneath the bleeding tree. She quickly averted her eyes and her thoughts. "You know Thomas, I think you might be right about this place. The structure seems the worse for wear."

"You guys think someone really demoed this place?" Max asked.

"It sure looks that way," Thomas replied as he took out his cellphone.

"What are you doing with that?" Emerlyn curiously inquired.

"I have a theory, and I figure it's worth a try," Thomas replied as he held up his phone and proceeded to snap a series of photos in all directions of the church. Max and Emerlyn nervously huddled around Thomas as he examined the photographs. Max could feel his pulse in his neck as his high-strung heart thumped harder in his chest.

"I don't see anything," Emerlyn murmured in confusion.

Thomas continued towards the altar and the obstructed cellar door at the far end of the church. He raised his camera to the eerie inverted cross that hung from the moldering wall and snapped another photo.

"Still nothing," Thomas said, his voice plagued with frustration.

"At this point, I can't tell if that's good news or bad news," Emerlyn muttered as she held her hand over her chest where the crucifix necklace hung. She half-expected that cross to be upside down, too.

"Hey, Bro. How are we supposed to get through that door, anyway?" Max asked as he pointed towards the rubble that covered the entrance to the undercroft.

Thomas reluctantly put away his phone and looked to his inquisitive brother. "There are more ways than one to skin a cat, Max."

"Awe, I hate that saying!" Emerlyn gagged audibly in the background.

"Yeah, I have to agree with Em on this one, Bro. That's not the best proverb you've ever used," Max crinkled his nose and tilted his head. Thomas rolled his eyes and ducked as he exited the church through a hole in the wall.

"Do you see that over there?" Thomas asked, pointing at a small, dilapidated building that lay directly behind the altar wall of the church. "That would be the church hall, and I'm betting there's another entrance to the undercroft."

Max poked his head through the hole in the wall and felt the sting of sunlight on his neck followed by the soothing chill of the autumn breeze. "Oh yay…I sure would be disappointed if we couldn't find the super secret door to the super, super creepy underground tunnel that leads to the even creepier ancient grimoire of death!" he exclaimed in a sort of monotone sarcasm.

The three entered the small wooden shack. Parts of it appeared to be charred in irregular patterns from a fire, possibly even from a bolt of lightning. Thomas's eyes traced the seared lines on the walls to another altar at the far end of the room. Above it, were various pagan symbols of protection including a pentagram.

"An altar and seals of protection. Are you thinking what I'm thinking?" Thomas turned to Emerlyn, taking a candid photo of her.

"Might as well have painted a giant X on the floor," Emerlyn replied as her eyes shifted from the altar to the dark shadow that skulked beneath it.

In that moment, Emerlyn found herself back in her grandmother's room, peering into the dismal abyss and knowing that the black void was still staring back at her. Whatever gift or curse she possessed, it had cost her more than it had ever given. It was why she never left her room without her crucifix, a symbol of protection more than a sign of faith. Sometimes, Emerlyn wondered if her grandmother suffered from the same plight, contemplating what she must have seen in her last few moments of life. Emerlyn lived in constant fear of what she might see next; or more accurately, what might see her next. It was time that this so-called gift was put to good use. That is why she agreed to help Thomas.

"Em? Em, are you ok?" Thomas snapped his fingers in front of Emerlyn's face. Her eyes were glazed over. "Em?"

"Yeah, of course. I was just thinking; that's all."

"What did you see Em?" Max asked timidly.

"Nothing. Nothing but accursed nihility," Emerlyn rubbed her eyes. "I'm fine though, really."

"Alright then. Can I get a little help moving this?" Thomas struggled to move the relatively large slabs of stone. Max and Emerlyn joined him on one end of the altar.

Once again, in true ceremonious fashion, the three counted aloud, "One, two, three!" The trio pushed with all their might, managing to force the reluctant altar into the corner of the room.

"Well, what do ya know, boys? Looks like we've got ourselves a genuine secret passage." Emerlyn tried her best to talk with an authentic cowgirl accent while winking and holding up two finger guns.

"It's just like Dr. Steven Greer said, 'Nothing critical is above the surface of the ground. It's either in space or it's underground.'" Thomas smiled as he wiped the sweat from his brow and straightened his glasses. His brother raised an eyebrow in confusion.

"Are you two seriously having another moment right now? I swear you are so fricken weird! You really deserve each other," Max shook his head in disbelief. "No more flirting today! We've reached the maximum amount of wooing that can take place in a fricken, haunted hollow!"

Thomas instinctively took a quick look at the photos on his phone, an obvious attempt to avoid his brother's embarrassing comments. It was clearly a generational coping mechanism, but this time there was an anomaly in one of the photographs. It was the same vivid corpse that hung, anathematized beneath the tree, presumably Amelia. Only this time, she lingered around Emerlyn. With one scabby, bleeding limb around Emerlyn's shoulders and the other pointing with a crooked, broken index finger towards Thomas, it seemed to take sudden notice of him. Horror-struck, he remained motionless and afraid for what seemed like an eternity.

"Anyone else feel a draft in here?" Emerlyn shivered from the unseen touch of Amelia.

"Yea, it's probably just from the undercroft." Thomas looked up from the phone, doing his best to hide the fear in his eyes as he broke free from a stupefied state of mind. There's no point in startling anyone by showing them the photo, he thought quietly to himself. But why was it pointing at me?

"I don't know. I can't help but feel like we're being watched," Emerlyn replied, still rubbing her arms for warmth. "The room feels so heavy. It's not the same as the cabin."

Still shaken by the picture, Thomas studied the correlation between Emerlyn's behavior and the phantom in the photo. In that moment, he caught a glimpse of the terrifying paranormal encounter she experienced in her grandmother's bedroom, finding himself in a fathomless ocean of fear and sadness. Thomas was no psychic medium, but with Emerlyn, he was sort of an empath. He could feel surge after surge of melancholy disgorging from Emerlyn's hemorrhaging heart. It was why he knew she was telling the truth in the car when she recounted her ghostly encounter; and it was why he knew she was lying when she told Max she felt fine.

Chapter 10

Thomas took the first step down the sandy stone stairs of the surreptitious passage. Unlike the over-glorified adventure films of Hollywood, there were no flickering torches, secret skylights, or any ancient, undisclosed technology awaiting them. There was only devilry and darkness in this tunnel of doom. Emerlyn used the small floodlight on her phone as she carefully followed Thomas and Max to the bottom of the shaft. The air was thick and musty, accompanied by the occasional plunk and plop sounds of dripping water in the distance. The crudely constructed walls were rough, uneven, and yielded a blood-red dust of levigating sandstone.

"Devils or otherwise, if there's a place to find cryptids, this is it," Thomas mumbled to himself while meticulously navigating the harrowing passage.

His eyes played tricks on him as they strained to adjust to the black void that ominously awaited. With every step forward, the rolling yellow and red irises of reptilian shapeshifters fluttered in the back of his mind. *Pull yourself together*, Thomas scolded himself internally. No more running. Every fiber of his being was screaming to leave the tunnel and just go home, but he refused to be the coward this time. Thomas repudiated the idea of being the claustrophobic fool that he was the night before.

"Hey, Bro," Max whispered to Thomas as they tiptoed deeper into the dispiriting pools of darkness. "So I was thinking about what you said last night. Ya' know the part about there being a creepy death cult out here?" His face was only partially illuminated by the glow of Emerlyn and Thomas's phones.

"Yea, I recall," Thomas replied sternly, attempting to conceal his shaky voice.

"Well, I was just thinking that we don't have Jack's wheel gun with us,"

Max paused for a moment, looking at the eldritch, crimson colored walls. "I know we've been a little preoccupied with this demon and ghost stuff, but what if we run into someone like that cannibal psycho, Albert Fish? I mean, that dude skinned kids alive and cooked them into broths and shit! We didn't even bring a damn knife! We're totally screwed."

"I don't think anyone's been down here for a long time, Max." Thomas placed his hand on his brother's shoulder and looked him in the eyes. "Don't let your imagination get the best of you. You don't want to end up a coward like me." Thomas had never spoken so plainly about himself, and the words stung a bit more than he'd expected. "But you're right. If we had a weapon, I'm sure we'd all feel a bit safer. I'm sorry."

"Well, congratulations!" Emerlyn interrupted. "Just when I thought this Halloween couldn't possibly get anymore macabre, you had to go and bring up cannibalism, Max!"

"Guys, just try and keep it together," Thomas interjected. "No one is getting cooked into a broth or barbecued today. We find the rest of the book, and we get out of here. Okay?"

Emerlyn and Max nodded in the pale, white glow of the small floodlights. The ceiling of the tunnel was significantly lower than the entrance, and the three hunched as they came to another pile of rubble.

"Just like the church." Emerlyn knelt down and shined her light around the edges of the obstruction. "I don't think we can get through this without the risk of collapsing the entire tunnel."

"Fuck!" Thomas yelled in frustration. His voice echoed throughout the undercroft; tiny pieces of rock crumbled from the amplitude. "You're right. There's no getting through."

Meanwhile, Max groaned and sighed in the background as he slouched against the cold tunnel wall. Suddenly, his back sunk deeper into the sandstone, and the large bricks began to shift. Before he could let out a whimper, he fell backwards and tumbled into a newly discovered cavity.

"Max! Where are you, Max?" Emerlyn screamed as she frantically darted across the tunnel, light in hand. Thomas quickly pivoted his posture, spinning around to face the wall on which his brother was leaning. "Thomas! There's a hole in the wall!" Emerlyn waved her hand, struggling to see through the thick cloud of red dust that filled the air. Without much thought for himself, Thomas charged through the vermilion haze.

"Ow!" Max exclaimed as he broke out into a dust-induced coughing fit. "You stepped on me, Bitch!"

"Max?" Thomas asked as he shined the light onto his own feet.

"Yea! Now could you please stop stepping on my friggin hand?" Max cursed as he held his hand in pain. "So much for pursuing my dream of being the world's most successful hand model."

"I'm sure you're going to be ok, Max." Emerlyn knelt down by his side, examining his fingers.

"I feel like you're not hearing me! My dreams of being the next J.P. Prewitt are fucking ruined, Em!" Max replied in the most serious of tones.

"Ok. Get up, Mr. Hand Model." Thomas reached out to help his brother recover from the fall. "Your hand looks fine to me."

"Easy for you to say with your beautiful, scab-free hands! Don't look at me. I'm hideous!" Max scolded as he scrambled back to his feet, aggressively dusting himself. He coughed and took out his inhaler. "I didn't even bring my moisturizing lotion. I wish Paige was here. She always has that Pumpkin Body Butter from Trader Joe's. Wait a minute. . .Did I just fall into a double-uber-super-secret passage?"

"Um, yea! It certainly appears that way," Thomas replied as he investigated their new surroundings. "It looks much older than the other tunnel. It looks ancient."

"All of this under a church? I'm starting to wonder if Christianity got it all wrong. What if we have our good guys and our bad guys all mixed up?" Emerlyn's eyes teared up. A bit of it was from fear, but most of it came from frustration. "All of the lies, the secrecy, the grimoire. . .It's all here, beneath a fucking church!"

"I don't think we're beneath the church, Em." Thomas held up his light and let out a loud, lengthy exhale. The secret room was no room at all. It was a cavernous hollow, not marked by the hands of ancient man like the Anasazi, but by the crooked, circuitous claws of the bleeding tree above. Crimson roots ran like a Mephistophelian plafond of throbbing arteries down from the center of the ceiling, weaving in and out of the red dome and sandstone walls like oxygenated capillaries of Hell. The rock floor was riddled with a mixture of seemingly nonsensical, tattoo-like carvings of foreign words, otherworldly shapes, and oddly familiar demoniacal calligraphy that captivated, fascinated, and bewitched their curious minds.

Max stooped down, dusting away debris from a portion of the floor. "Renich Viasa Avage Lilith Lirach."

Emerlyn proceeded to read from a separate piece nearby, "Es Na Ayer Abbadon Avage."

"No! Stop!" Thomas commanded. "Don't read any of it aloud! This place wa-was not built by hu-humans!" Panic-stricken, Thomas stuttered his words as he turned his light towards Max and Emerlyn. "A demon sleeps beneath the bleeding tree; and here we are, beneath the fucking tree!" Thomas took a deep breath in an effort to slow his thoughts. "Those words and symbols on the ground are demonic enns. I'm pretty sure you just read invocations of Abaddon and Lilith. Reading anything in this room puts us all at risk." Thomas secretly wondered why Amelia's spirit would be connected to such an awful place if she was truly innocent. Perhaps she was a witch after all, Thomas thought to himself.

"Who?" Max asked as he struggled to keep his voice and his phone-light from trembling.

"Not who, but what and where." Thomas corrected his brother. "Lilith is depicted as a female demon of darkness who's said to have been Adam's first wife. On the other hand, Abaddon is both a place of destruction and an angel of the abyss."

"Abyss, did you say?" Emerlyn felt her vision pulsate with every jarring thud of her heavy heart. As she lost herself in the void, she found herself back in her grandmother's room once again. Creak. Crack. Creak. Crack. The sound of the old rocking chair replayed in her head, and then the thud of heavy footsteps walking towards her. What was it? Was Amelia the witch Holcomb claimed?

"Abyss. Yea, like Hell. Ya know?" Thomas replied to Emerlyn while he shifted his attention to the center of the chamber and snapped another photograph.

Invisible to the naked eye, a frayed rope stained in blood and ichor dangled from the center of the ceiling like some sort of morbid chandelier. The soiled line hovered, mere inches above the tattooed floor, where a horridly beaten girl laid in a pool of her own bodily fluids. Thomas gasped and quickly took another photograph, but the girl was gone. Instead, he saw the words, 'Destroy the page', crudely written across the floor in illusory clumps of clotted blood and mangled scraps of human flesh.

The gore was smeared over a large disc-shaped symbol in the center of the floor containing a grotesque pentacle that appeared to be a primitive representation of the one found on the grimoire page. Emerlyn and Max examined the photos and were left with horrified expressions.

"So after Holcomb and the townspeople had Amelia executed and buried, someone dug her up and brought her body down here to be mutilated?" Emerlyn gagged on every word as she fought back the sudden urge to vomit.

"This has to be the place where it all started. The Dream Demon once slept beneath the bleeding tree but was summoned or disturbed here. It seems to me that the invocator didn't fully understand the evil they unleashed. Maybe the events that followed were supposed to serve as some sort of blood ritual to appease the afreets inscribed on the floor? Why would the pentagram from the grimoire be carved into the floor?" Thomas rubbed his forehead as he felt a severe tension headache start to overcome him. "And there's a warning to destroy the page that we discovered in the cabin. But why would she have it hidden away if she wanted it destroyed?"

"It's hard to trust anything we've seen. How do we even know we're communicating with the same spirit? Whoever did this had to be the one responsible for burying Holcomb alive," Emerlyn replied as she gently put her hand on the back of Thomas's neck in an effort to ease his stress headache. "Maybe things started to get out of control as they performed more rituals from the spellbook. Burying Holcomb seems like a last-ditch effort to stop the affliction, which is synonymous with the suicide dybbuk and the Dream Demon."

"So when the devil worshipers finally realized that devil worshipping was a bad idea, they did more devil-worship-stuff like mutilating a corpse for Lilith and Abaddon just to try and stop a different demon?" Max crinkled his nose at Emerlyn and Thomas. "Now, a ghost-thingy has the nerve to tell us not to keep the grimoire page? Makes sense…"

"The rest of the book must contain passages that suggest the user has some sort of control over the Dream Demon that is released," Thomas replied, a perplexed look on his face. "My guess is that the user–or-users–assumed they would be immune to the evil they unleashed. Something changed their mind. Maybe the page we have is filled with more lies than truth. Maybe that's why we were told to destroy it."

"Do you think any other entities were actually released? Maybe they were put back in their places with the use of the book and the blood ritual." Emerlyn continued to examine the demonic enns on the ground. "I mean, who knows what is written on the other pages of the book!"

"Perhaps the suicide dybbuk, or Dream Demon, was just more difficult to control; and therefore, harder to put to rest," Thomas interjected. "I don't think the other spirits conjured here had nearly as much influence over the townspeople. I mean, you guys read from the floor and nothing happened, yet." Thomas massaged the bridge of his nose in order to combat the onset of the intense headache. "The pentacle and disc must be more significant than we realize. The grimoire page contains six descriptions of suicides and six corresponding depictions of death on the pentacle. Maybe, the symbol was used as an instruction manual to fully awaken the demon. It could have been used as some sort of metaphysical conduit between unsuspecting members of Holcomb's flock and the demon. Maybe it allowed the Dream Demon to infect its host more easily? Now, what sort of disc shaped object would come into contact with all loyal churchgoers? The only thing that comes to mind is some sort of mock eucharist," Thomas paused, struggling to free his mind of the cluttered mess of clues. "Wait a minute! Do you guys remember Mrs. C.'s theory about everyone getting sick from the bread at the church?" Thomas's eyes shifted up and to the left as he continued to collect his thoughts. "This chamber could have been used to conduct a form of spirit cooking in order to expedite the full awakening of the demon."

"Spirit cooking?" Emerlyn narrowed her eyes in confusion.

"It's the disgusting practice of making ceremonial wafers that sort of serve as a mock eucharist. Aleister Crowley called them the Cake of Light. The wafers were often made from oil, honey, menstrual blood, and... sperm," Thomas paused to hold back the puke that had forcefully made its way into his throat. The thought alone made him nauseated. "Other recipes called for breast milk, fresh morning piss, and obviously more blood."

"Thomas, are you telling me that someone was making a mock Eucharist down here with a concoction of bodily fluids and feeding it to Reverend Holcomb and his flock?" Emerlyn ran her fingers through her hair, squinting her eyes in scepticism.

"Look, I know it sounds crazy, but think about it. Amelia didn't participate in any of the church functions, least of all consuming human excrement. Mr. C.'s story made that part very clear," Thomas intejected.

"First of all, I just want to say ew! Second, that's an awful lot of puzzle pieces to connect. Every time we discover another clue, I feel more confused." Max's crestfallen eyes widened with uncertainty.

"It's become overwhelming for us, Thomas." Emerlyn put her arm around Max in an effort to comfort him.

"Don't give up now, guys! Look. So far, it appears that Holcomb was a shitty person but ultimately probably not a devil worshiper. It sounds to me like he was trying to hide the grimoire under the church in an effort to stop the evil from spreading. I don't think he even knew about this secret chamber. It looks like he was trying to protect the town. He only went after Amelia because he saw her leave the church cellar with a page from the book."

"Okay, I'm with you so far," Emerlyn nodded in agreement.

"We still have an unknown perpetrator, someone who was close enough to the reverend to fly under the radar," Thomas continued. "This person was responsible for essentially poisoning the townspeople to spread fear and death; and I'm betting Mrs. C. was right about it being some sort of foul bread in place of the body of Christ. It seems very likely that they were also responsible for coaxing Holcomb into executing Amelia. We've all assumed that the reverend saw precisely what Amelia had in her hand, because we were investigating from her point of view. The evildoer could've just as easily convinced Holcomb that she had actually stolen the entire book. All the while, the unknown perpetrator hid the grimoire in this secret chamber in an attempt to return the demon to its realm."

"That's one hell of a theory." Max raised his eyebrows as he continued to fiddle with his injured hand. "So Amelia took the page because she was also trying to stop the dybbuk?"

"She must've thought that there was no other way to stop it. Once Amelia was caught stealing the page, she became the perfect scapegoat; but it looks like the hanging had no effect on the dybbuk. It appears only certain methods can entrap the demon. Unfortunately, it looks like she just got caught in the middle of an inter-dimensional turf war," Thomas replied. "From her point of view, Holcomb was probably enemy number one. She was in way over her head, and it killed her."

"But why? What's it all for?" Emerlyn maintained a tone of skepticism. "I just don't see it. What if Amelia really was a witch? What if she released the suicide dybbuk?"

"Why does anyone do terrible things?" Thomas's tone of despair seemed to burn a hole right through the center of Emerlyn's heart. "The inscriptions on the floor, blood rituals under the tree, and unleashing a demon onto an unsuspecting community seems an awful lot like a form of Luciferianism. It could even predate modern satanic cult practices. The goal?" Thomas reexamined the incantations in the chamber. "It could be as simple as trying to satiate a lust for power over the locals, but more likely this was a near successful attempt to open a direct line of communication with the devil or a portal straight to Hell. It just seems like the dybbuk that crawled through the inter-dimensional rift had no desire to play by the rules. Even if Amelia was the original invocator, I'm not sure it mattered in the end. Things quickly spiraled out of control, and someone else got involved, someone that doesn't shy away from murder and mutilating corpses."

"Alright, I think I'm still with you," Emerlyn paused for a moment. "It would actually make sense if Amelia was the original summoner of the dybbuk. It would better explain how she had knowledge of the burial ritual page. Like you said, I'm not sure it mattered in the end. So after Amelia's sacrifice, at least one other practitioner who had knowledge of the ritual page hunted for the suicide dybbuk's next host?" Emerlyn sighed, cleared her throat, and then straightened her posture. "You said that this person was flying under Holcomb's radar, so they had to have been close friends? Acquaintances? When the demon finally attached itself to the reverend, it must have been a difficult decision to bury him alive."

"I don't know Em," Max answered. "Sounds like they were pretty demented and desperate. Everyone who had contact with that spellbook either died or became a murderer."

"All the more reason for us to find the rest of the grimoire before it gets into the wrong hands, again." Emerlyn replied, swallowing the bitter acid that seeped up from her nervous stomach. "There has to be a better way of removing this thing from our plane of existence."

"It might already be too late," Thomas cautioned. "Our fates may already be sealed."

"Even if we do find the rest of the book, what good will it do against the dybbuk?" Max asked apprehensively, hoping that Thomas or Emerlyn would have a comforting answer. "From what you've said, it seems like the book just doesn't work on the Dream Demon. We're not going to bury anyone alive, are we?"

"Max! Of course not!" Emerlyn gasped. "I'm sure your brother will find a way. He knows more about the occult and paranormal than anyone I've ever met," she paused. "We'll find a way, Max."

"One step at a time," Thomas mumbled under his breath, half talking to himself. "I just need to see the complete puzzle. I need to have all the pages in front of me. There has to be something that they missed."

Chapter 11

"Mr. and Mrs. Carter, thank you for your cooperation. I'm Deputy Huey." The deputy sheriff took off his hat and nodded as he entered the living room area. "I was informed that you spoke with my colleagues at the hospital. I'm very sorry to hear about your son."

"It's no problem at all, Huey." Mr. C. forced half a grin, purposely omitting his law enforcement title. Over the years he'd lost all faith in government, especially LE. "It's been so overwhelming that we haven't even thought of checking our security cameras. Please, have a seat. I'll bring up the infrared footage from last night." Huey took a seat near the computer while Mr. C. brought up the video. "Of course, I'll be making a copy for your records."

"Much obliged, Mr. Carter," Deputy Huey replied as he took a quick visual survey of the room, noticing various Halloween trinkets and tasteful decor; but something else caught his eye. "That's quite a nice library of relics you have here, Mr. Carter. Some of these books look like they could be museum pieces."

"I doubt very seriously that any museum could ever value my books as much as I do." Mr. C. turned from the computer and glanced contemplatively at his bookshelves. "Besides, it's not the antiquated nature that makes them valuable to me; it's the content." Mr. C. shifted in his chair and turned towards the deputy. "Find anything else of interest in my house?"

"Actually, I was also going to compliment your gun collection and the cross-stand of body armor in the den area. Your gear is probably better than the department's." Huey squinted while returning the half-grin that he'd previously received from Mr. C.

"Thanks for noticing. I'm surprised you didn't refer to it as an arsenal,

Huey. That seems to be the latest buzz word when referring to an American citizen's gun collection." Mr. C. chuckled as he pivoted back towards the computer screen.

"Would either of you like some warm tea or coffee?" Mrs. C. habitually used offerings of hospitality to mask her nervousness. "I find it quite cold in here."

"No thank you, ma'am. I'm fine," Huey answered politely. "So are these cameras motion activated, or is it a continuous feed?"

"We have two cameras currently installed, one on Jack's side of the house, and one recording the driveway. Both are motion activated," Mr. C. responded, annoyed. "Here we go. There are a few short clips from last night. This one is Jack driving up way after curfew." Mr. C.'s tone changed to one of disappointment, but he was not surprised. "This one, though, is interesting…" his voice trailed off, and he leaned towards the computer screen.

Mrs. C. held her hands over her chest in anticipation. The camera near Jack's window suddenly activated and began to flicker. The image quality is poor and unusually grainy.

"Now why would a motion-activated IR camera suddenly turn on if nothing's there?" Huey asked as he squinted his eyes, leaning closer to the screen. "Is it a glitch or some kind of equipment failure?"

"Huey, I assure you it's no failure on my part. I take my family's security very seriously. These cameras have always been one hundred percent reliable," Mr. C. protested Huey's insulting hypothesis. "They are always crystal clear. There must be some sort of outside interference. I hear they've been rolling out 5G tech nationwide, causing weird anomalies and unexplained power outages. The military industrial complex is always experimenting with things they do not understand, and we are the test subjects. I'm not convinced that this fifth generation mobile network is safe." Mr. C. shook his head in disapproval and continued to mutter curse words under his breath. "I hear you can even steer hurricanes these days."

"Look, there's movement in Jack's window!" Mrs. C. interjected.

"What's the time stamp on this footage?" The deputy asked from behind Mr. C.'s shoulder, ignoring his blatant accusations of government misconduct.

"It says 3:33 am. Curious," Mr. C. mumbled in disbelief.

"Does the time strike you as odd or significant, Mr. Carter?" Huey did his best to be patient and civil with Mr. C.

"Well, since you've inquired. Some of the locals say that 3:33 AM is an angelic hour that is a mark of protection and importance. Others say it's the true witching hour. Considering today's date, I'd say the timing is pretty significant. My son and I have grown to be quite reverential of superstitions, deputy. He'd know better than to go wandering off at an hour like that."

"Oh, cut the shit, Philip Carter! This is no time for more of your ghost stories and conspiracy theories. This is our son!" his wife scolded. She knew he hated the name Philip. It was passed down from his great-great grandfather, and she only used it when she wished her words to sting.

"The curtain seems to be fluttering." Huey pointed at the video. "There! The window is opening, and someone is crawling out with a gun."

"That's Jack. What are you doing, Son?" Mr. C.'s heart was racing behind his deceptively calm demeanor. It wasn't credulity, but he'd tried his best to instill a respect for unspoken rules and superstitions in his son. The footage of Jack's behavior was disheartening. Perhaps Mrs. C. was right about his ghost stories being inappropriate for Jack and his friends.

"It looks like he's talking to someone, but I can't tell if anyone's really there." Huey's voice broke as he cleared the lump of fear from his throat. "One of his hands appears to be bandaged; the other is holding a revolver. All the while he's talking to someone who isn't there? Does your son have problems with sleepwalking?"

"No, never." Mr. C.'s eyes widened as he continued to watch the video. "Here's where the camera near the driveway starts recording." The footage was substantially grainier and flickered more frequently than the previous clip.

"So this is when he wandered into the garage," Huey mumbled. "What's the time stamp on this?"

"Impossible…" Mr. C. leaned back in his chair. "The time still says 3:33 AM. It's as if the time on this camera is around three minutes behind. My cameras have never lagged before."

"That's an awful lot of threes in one night. Are you sure no one has tampered with this footage?"

"Deputy Huey, I assure you, no one has touched this fucking footage until now," Mr. C. protested. "No one knows about these cameras, not even Jack. Only my wife and I have the password to this computer."

"Alright, alright. I'm just trying to help. That's all."

"I'm sorry, Mr. Huey. As you can imagine, my husband and I are processing quite a lot of stressful information," Mrs. C. interrupted. "So far, this security footage has raised more questions than it's answered. You'll have to excuse our tempers. It's just hard seeing our son acting so unusual."

"Yes, of course. Is this the end of the surveillance?" Deputy Huey turned his attention from Mrs. C. back to the computer.

"The remaining clip shows my wife and me rushing Jack to the hospital. Before you even ask, the time stamp is 3:40 AM. As soon as we heard the gunshot, we searched the house. Somewhere along the way, the time must have corrected itself," Mr. C. preemptively answered the deputy's predictable questions. "However, it seems that the camera near Jack's window was triggered again. It happened at 4:00 AM."

"That's twenty minutes after we left the house!" Mrs. C. gasped as she covered her mouth.

"There appears to be a female walking haltingly through your yard." Huey leaned closer to the screen. "She looks severely injured. Her clothes are covered in blood and--is that a Goddamn rope around her neck?" The image began to distort until it was no longer possible to see the female figure. Bewildered, the deputy stood up and paced around the room with his hands on his hips. "Look, this kind of shit is way above my paygrade!" Huey paused in the center of the room to collect himself. The warm rays of persimmon sunlight illuminated one side of his face while the cold blue hue from the computer monitor enveloped the other.

"Try and relax, Deputy. It's Halloween, remember?" Mr. C. shook his head at Huey. "It's probably just some dumb kid from school trying to prank our son. It could be completely unrelated."

Huey turned his attention back to the computer screen. The figure suddenly reappeared through the pulsating flashes of distortion. "Mr. Carter, that dumb kid just climbed into your son's window." Huey's voice began to shake as he stared at the grainy, flickering footage of the unidentified female, inelastically crawling through the open window and disappearing from the camera. "Just curious, is there any footage showing the individual leaving your home?"

"The only other time the cameras were triggered was when we drove up with you." Mr. C.'s eyes wandered around the room, and the hairs on the back of his neck tingled.

Deputy Huey put his dominant hand on his pistol and quietly placed his index finger over his lips. He leaned towards Mr. C.'s ear, quietly asking him to point the way to Jack's room.

Huey took vanguard, tiptoeing down the hallway. He couldn't help but assume that the girl in the window had something to do with Jack's incident and the cameras' malfunctions. Mr. C. quietly removed his carry pistol from his waistband and followed closely behind, carefully shielding his wife. The stiff, hardwood floors creaked with every hesitant step forward, the air carried a bitter chill as it breathed through the hallway; and Mrs. C.'s eyes watered with fear as she watched the dimming orange glow from the living room fall further and further behind her.

Huey pointed his gun and flashlight inside the first doorway, quickly scanning the small room. "Bathroom's clear," he turned and whispered to Mr. and Mrs. C. as they kept an eye down the hall.

Mrs. C. couldn't help but keep her head on a swivel, constantly feeling the need to check behind them. She detested the feeling of being scared and never found the least bit of enjoyment in horror movies or her husband's terrorizing tall tales. Currently, she was loathing everything about this Halloween.

"Next room's Jack's," Mr. C. whispered to the deputy as he pointed at Jack's doorway.

It was closed, but a pitch-black silhouette pirouetted unsteadily through the natural lighting that seeped from under the door. Its edges, blurred and semi-translucent. Its movements, erratic and extremely unnerving.

"What the hell?" Huey muttered under his breath. The dizzying display of the penumbra, married to the shadow, continued to dance through the bleeding light. As he reached the room, he cleared his throat and placed one hand on the doorknob while holding his pistol in the other. "Listen up! If anyone is still in there, identify yourself! I'm in the middle of an active investigation!" he paused. The shadow cast under the door halted. The air was hauntingly still; and so, too, was the shadow. "We know you're in there! We're coming in!" Like clockwork, Huey rushed through the door, checking forward and right flank, while Mr. C. took left flank.

"It's empty," Mrs. C. mumbled as she clumsily entered the room behind her husband, "but what we saw under the door..."

"Just the wind," Deputy Huey remarked as he stroked the dark, red curtain that began to flutter over Jack's window. "I guess the window was never closed, but that still doesn't explain the girl. Could she have gone out the back? Maybe she evaded your surveillance."

"Not likely," Mr. C. replied. "We have an exceptionally tall fence behind and around the other side of the house. She'd need to carry around a pretty big ladder to get over that thing. Anyone who enters or exits the property has to do so within the range of my security cameras."

Huey scratched his head and holstered his weapon as he stared out the open window. The tepid rays of sunlight stung his fair skin, and the cool breeze nipped at his ears and nose. It was calming, almost serene.

Mrs. C. hurriedly approached the window; but an ice-cold gust of wind ripped through the room, violently slamming shut both the window and the bedroom door behind her. She let out a blood-curdling scream and fell backwards, landing in the deputy's arms. The momentum of the fall knocked Huey backwards, causing him to tip over the nightstand near Jack's bed. Its contents spilled onto the floorboards. Instinctively, Mr. C. rushed to his wife's side, quickly removing her from Huey's embrace.

"Are you okay, Dear?" Mr. C. asked, suspiciously eyeing the deputy who was busy collecting Jack's phone, knife, and keys from the floor.

Huey paused for a moment when he noticed Jack's phone had accidentally illuminated from the fall. The lock screen was a photo of Jack and what appeared to be his girlfriend.

"Curious," he mumbled. She looked nothing like the girl in the security footage. So if he wasn't messing around with his girlfriend last night, then who? he thought to himself. Admittedly, it would be hard to identify anyone dressed up in that kind of costume; if, indeed, it was a costume at all. He returned the items to the nightstand and turned his attention to the window. "What the hell is that?"

Huey pointed towards a tiny, green gremlin with large, soulless black eyes, standing ominously at the far end of the lawn, holding an ammo pouch filled with crispy chicken nuggets. It stared at the three of them in the window; and then madly darted into the bushes, emitting a high-pitched shrill that seemed to perforate through the walls.

"Let's see them aliens!" a slightly muffled voice yawped in the distance. "Yeet!"

"Those fucking kids and their Area 51 jokes! Let the meme die, already! No one even came close to sneaking into the base!" Mrs. C. exclaimed. "And speaking of dying, what did I tell you about fixing these Goddamn windows, Philip? One day, they're going to give me a heart attack!"

"With everything that's happened today, I wouldn't be surprised if we just witnessed an actual extraterrestrial all hopped up on Halloween candy." Deputy Huey's voice was awash with emotional exhaustion. "I can't imagine what the two of you are going through, right now. Mr. Carter, I know I haven't earned your trust; but I will do my best to get to the bottom of your son's incident." The deputy took a deep breath and turned from the window, making eye contact with Mr. C. "It's been an extremely taxing day for your family, and I know you've more important things to do than chat with me. I'll take a copy of the surveillance footage, and head back to the station."

Mr. C. nodded and turned to open the bedroom door. "Ya know Hunnie, I think you were right about needing something warm to drink. Before we head back to the hospital, would you like to join me for a cup of tea? It'll take a few minutes to copy the footage for Huey." It was not just a small peace offering to his wife but a genuine gesture of love.

"Actually, Dear, I think I'll have coffee," she managed a slight smirk.

"Yes, ma'am. Coming right up." Mr. C. reached for his wife's hand, and they headed down the hall. Huey followed, settling near the computer as he patiently waited for the video download to complete.

"All done here." Deputy Huey poked his head into the kitchen. "If anything else comes up, call me," he said, handing his personal phone number to Mr. C. "I'll have a couple of my colleagues patrol the area while you're away with your son. I don't know where the trespasser went, but we'll find her. I promise; we'll get to the bottom of this, all of it," he paused, adjusting the brim of his hat. "Well, maybe not all of it. I don't know if we'll ever find out the truth about that green alien."

Mr. C. looked at his wife and grinned, "But I want to believe." He nudged her with his elbow before shaking the deputy's hand. "We'll be sure to call if we see or hear anything else. Thank you for your assistance, Huey. Alice, I guess we better drive separately to the hospital in case one of us is needed at the station. Page won't be around to take care of Jack this evening, and we can't leave him alone." Mr. C. looked to his wife as she nodded in agreement.

Chapter 12

Thomas and Max took extra care to reseal the secret chamber under the tree while Emerlyn held the light in the tunnel. Thomas took one last glimpse of the demonic enns, the Eucharistic pentacle, and the devilish, finger-like roots that cradled the crimson walls of the claret-colored room before wedging the stone door in place. He looked at Emerlyn through the cold, white glow of her cellphone and said the words Max was so desperately longing to hear. "Let's get the eff out of here."

The trio footslogged down the treacherous tunnel, up the stone stairs, and into the dilapidated building hidden behind the church. They did their best to place the altar exactly as they'd found it, hoping that no one else would discover the hidden passage beneath it. As they made their way into the warm light of the sun, Thomas noticed its position in the sky.

"Not to sound like a boy scout again, but we're losing daylight pretty quickly," he said, gesturing towards the heavens.

"And still no book. Not to mention, we have no idea when, where, or who this thing will attack next," Emerlyn remarked, dusting her clothes underneath the orange glow of the fading, autumn sun. Thomas slouched in defeat as the three walked past the decrepit church, purposely avoiding the ebony murder of crows that noisily nested atop the blistered, bleeding tree.

"Not to give a false sense of hope, but I have a hypotenuse!" Max proudly declared.

"A hypotenuse?" Emerlyn teased. "You mean a hypothesis?"

"Em, that's what I said. Try to keep up, okay?" Max retorted. "So whoever knew about the book and the rituals must have been very close to Holcomb, right?"

"Yea, we said that already, Max," Thomas answered, literally facepalming his reply.

"Whoa! Now, that facepalm was hurtful; but I'm gonna let it slide." Max authoritatively pointed his index finger at Thomas. "So this person buried Holcomb alive, but what happened to this mystery person when they died?"

"Um, they were probably buried by the surviving townspeople." Emerlyn raised an eyebrow while tilting her head.

"And where might a close friend or relative be buried?" Max interrogated the two as he shifted the target of his index finger from Thomas to Holcomb's gravesite.

"They'd literally be close." Thomas grinned at his brother. "Especially if the remaining town folk had no idea about the Dream Demon ritual or who performed it. Max, are you telling me you are coming out of retirement? You little graverobber."

"Not so fast, cowboys. How about we settle for reading the surrounding headstones, first." Emerlyn suggested as she and the boys started towards the crumbling, forgotten graveyard. "Let's try and make this quick. This is the last place on earth that I want to be after sundown."

It was Halloween, the veil was thin, and she could feel Amelia's constant presence in the hollow. Or was she sensing something else entirely? Even worse, she could feel the darkness from the plagued page inside her pocket growing stronger and stronger as the sun sank lower and lower.

"Agreed." Thomas straightened his posture and hastened his pace down the rocky wagon trail.

Max was already pulling ahead, and Emerlyn was moving swiftly beside him. Their haste was partly due to the sense of impending doom that dusk would bring and partly instinctual as they felt the hairs on the backs of their necks tingle from the very thought of the church and the tree watching their every move. It was all they could do to ignore the incessant caws from the crows in that decrepit tree. Harder still to disregard the creaks and cracks that emanated from the maniacal, superannuated church.

"These headstones are in bad shape." Max frowned as he examined the area in close proximity to Holcomb. "The inscriptions are shallow and weathered, but this one has a hammer symbol on it. Looks like it says Ellis Havely; I can't read much else."

"Maybe he was the local carpenter or blacksmith," Emerlyn chimed in. "Ya know, because the hammer symbol? If they took the time to engrave it, it must be significant."

Thomas nodded in agreement and examined another headstone near Holcomb that lay in ruins. He stared thoughtfully at the jagged shapes, rearranging them horizontally like craggy pieces of a puzzle.

"Em, Max…" Thomas's voice broke as his eyes began to water. The stones read:

HERE LIES PHILIP CARTER
CONFRACTUS PANEM

"Break bread…" Emerlyn's voice shook as she translated the Latin phrase that she'd often heard during Holy Communion. It truly hurt her heart to see her catechized belief system tied to such odious perversions in the hollow.

"Wait, a minute! Why would Jack's dad have his name on an old grave?" Max inquired. "Please, don't tell me he's a time traveler."

"It's generational," Thomas replied. His eyes burned at the sight of it. "The name must have been passed down from his great-great-grandfather." His voice shuddered with horror. Even in the subtle warmth of daylight, the crooked shards of Philip Carter's greying gravestone sent a haunting, wintry chill straight through the center of Thomas's evanescing soul. "Something isn't right, guys. We shouldn't be here."

Emerlyn and Max suddenly got the feeling that Mr. C. was now a prime suspect. In hindsight, the clues were there all along. He knew an awful lot about the events that transpired, even if some of the details were wrong. Wrong or omitted? Emerlyn's mind was racing; she was questioning everything. He had admitted to venturing into the hollow as a teen, but failed to mention discovering a headstone bearing his family name.

"We should tell Paige," Max suggested.

"Right. I'll text her," Emerlyn agreed.

"No," Thomas cautioned. "We don't want to leave a trail of text messages about this weird shit. Especially not if anyone suspects foul play with Jack's incident. We might all be under investigation."

"So maybe a simple phone call inquiring where she might be?" Emerlyn proposed.

"Yea, keep it light on the details until we find her." Thomas nodded, as he began walking towards the trail that would take them back to his mother's vehicle. Emerlyn and Max followed as she made the call.

"Paige? Yea, we're alright…Just wanted to let you know we're leaving… You're still with Jack? I'm so sorry…I'm sure it's only a matter of time before he wakes up, Paige…Okay, we'll meet ya there."

Chapter 13

The autumn sun was getting low, and its brilliant celestial display of cerise fire bursting through the metallic blinds was a painful contrast to the pale, sterile glow of the grim hospital lights that hung in despondency above Jack's bed. It was the last sunset of October; Paige prayed that it wasn't the last for Jack. She dreaded having to leave him tonight, but she knew the Devil's deal. If she didn't go, they'd come for her and rip her away from his side. No matter what, she swore it'd be the last Halloween she'd ever have to make a deal like that again. And just like clockwork, her phone buzzed in her pocket. She'd received the ill-tempered text that commanded her presence. It wasn't the Devil after all, but her black-hearted wretch of a mother was close enough. The abrupt, tingling surge of anger and sadness that warped her heart and clouded her mind was suddenly interrupted by a light knock at the door.

She turned around, half-expecting to see Emerlyn and the boys; but instead was greeted softly by Mrs. C.'s kind voice.

"Hi, Paige. We're sorry it took a little longer than expected with the deputy. Thank you so much for staying by Jack's side."

"There's no other place I'd rather be." Paige's red eyes began to water, again. "Unfortunately, my parents are making me go home now."

"It's okay, Paige." Mr. C. put his hand on her shoulder and looked her in the eyes. "We know where your heart lies, and Jack does, too. Go home, get some rest, maybe have a little fun, and we'll call you when Jack wakes. He will wake up, Paige. It's important for us to believe that." Mr. C.'s eyes teared up; he hugged Paige as she began to sob in his arms. Mrs. C. sniffled in the background as she placed her hand on Jack's and looked at her baby boy lying in bed, only half alive. Little did she know, he was soon to have a baby of his own.

Paige lovingly kissed Jack's forehead and reluctantly exited the room. As she started down the bright corridor towards the elevator, she passed the snack room and the vending machine where Max had his epic battle for a protein shake. I'll have to call the guys when I get to the car. She reminded herself that her friends were on their way to meet her and wondered what they'd discovered in the hollow. Em and the boys had been gone all day; Paige hadn't even noticed until now. As the rickety elevator noisily descended to the parking garage, she wondered what kind of special horrors awaited her at the party. It was sad to think that she felt like an intruder, a stranger in her own home.

Paige opened the door to her mother's SUV, and a pair of glaring headlights rapidly approached her. As it drew nearer, her vision blurred into two uncomfortably bright halos of white light.

"Turn off your brights! You're blinding her!" Paige recognized the sound of Max's voice yelling from inside the car.

"Sorry, Paige!" Thomas apologized as he dimmed the headlights and killed the engine.

The orange incandescent glow of the overhead lamps eerily flickered above the dust and grime that was frenetically stirred by the frenzied vehicle. Paige's eyes struggled to adjust to the ill-lit, hazy atmosphere that currently clouded the parking garage.

"It's okay." Paige coughed out her words as she wafted the dust away from her face. "I was just about to call you guys. With everything that's happened, I lost track of time. I feel so fucking terrible about leaving, but my parents are making me go home to get ready for tonight."

"Wait, Paige." Emerlyn quickly hopped out of the passenger seat, making her way through the filth-ridden haze. "There are some things you must know before you leave. We don't have all the answers, but…" Emerlyn swallowed the lump of hesitation stubbornly lodged in the back of her throat. "We found Mr. C.'s name on a grave." Emerlyn's eyes watered; she stared into Paige's ever widening pupils as they rapidly adjusted to the darkness that blanketed them, but more importantly, calibrating the wicked implications that lurked behind the sinister tone of Emerlyn's every syllable. "We don't know exactly what it means, but…"

"Paige!" a voice called from a distance. An obdurate curtain of burnt orange filth still lingered beneath the scintillating garage lights, obscuring the speaker's identity.

Paige sank back into the driver's seat of her mother's SUV, shielding herself behind the half-open door. She anxiously gripped the steering wheel, shifting her line of sight between her friends and the direction of the summoning voice.

"Hey, I'm glad I caught you before you left! You forgot your purse in the room. We can't have you driving around without a license, now can we?" Mr. C. grinned as he stepped into view, handing Paige her belongings. "Oh, hey, kids! You here to see Jack?" The four of them stared blankly back at Mr. C. "Everything alright?" He could feel the fear seeping through their frozen, rigid postures and oozing from their wide-eyed expressions.

"We found your name on a vandalized headstone in the hollow!" Max yelled from behind Emerlyn. He couldn't hold it in any longer. "It was completely shattered, man! Last night, we investigated your ghost story. I never even got to hear it, so I thought it was complete horseshit. But we caught a ghost on camera! It was a girl hanging from the tree just like Amelia! We only went back there today because I found this Bible in Holcomb's grave after Thomas fell inside. I know I shouldn't have taken it, but I did. And then Jack ended up in the hospital, because he apparently released some kind of dark energy when he helped my brother. At first, we thought the Bible was cursed, so we wanted to put it back; but Holcomb wrote a passage inside that mentioned a grimoire. Turns out, the grimoire was another creepy book that talked about this suicide-dybbuk-Dream-Demon-thingy..."

"Max shut up!" Thomas drove his elbow into his brother's side. "Don't listen to him Mr. C. He's, ugh...he's had one of those big protein shakes today with tons of caffeine and sugar and stuff..."

"No, it's true, Mr. C." Emerlyn's voice cracked under the pressure. "I saw your name with my own eyes. Thomas pieced the headstone back together. There was this silhouetted apparition that seemed to be leading me around the hollow last night and another today. I thought it was Amelia, but I can't be sure. This morning, Max found an old cabin filled with bats; and when we were trying to escape, I found a page from some kind of spellbook. But I'm not sure that I really found it on my own. I think a spirit led me to it!" She shoved her hand into her pocket, relieved to finally share the inexplicable burden of the artifact with someone else. Thomas's fingers trembled nervously. He wiped the sweat from his brow as Emerlyn continued. "See? Amelia Groeh! Her name is right there!"

Bewildered, Mr. C. took the wrinkled page from Emerlyn, slowly digesting the repulsive imagery depicted, its morbid instructions, the leathery skin-like feel of it, and the handwriting of Amelia Groeh. The girl in the security footage...He thought to himself as he attempted to piece the clues together. Someone desecrated grandfather's grave. . .My son is hospitalized...Six deaths and a pentagram? Fragmented thoughts and questions raced through his head. Paige stood beside him, equally disturbed, but even more confused.

"Mr. C., we think Jack was attacked because Holcomb's grave contained the suicide dybbuk. There were fingernail marks and extensive damage on the inside of the coffin. It indicates a live burial, just like the one described on the page you're holding." Thomas stepped forward and adjusted his glasses. "We also believe that your great-great-grandfather, Philip Carter, may have initiated and orchestrated the events in your story. Holcomb wasn't the bad guy, and Amelia may actually have been a witch. There's a secret chamber embedded within the root system! The floor is covered in demonic enns and symbolism. Whether it was intentional or not, that's where we think Amelia may have awoken the evil spirit with the help of your ancestor. Mrs. C. was right! It was the bread in the church that sickened the townspeople! It was like a spiritual conduit that weakened their immune systems, allowing sickness and hysteria to spread like the plague. The bread was likely used as a tool to manipulate Holcomb into sacrificing Amelia. Maybe it was a genuine effort on your grandfather's part to stop the demon as it grew too powerful to control." Thomas took a long deep breath and exhaled slowly. "The only question now is, where's the spellbook? We need it in order to find another way to stop this thing. Without it, the only solution on that page seems...like murder."

"When the veil is thin, the suicide dybbuk can be released from its tomb," Mr. C. muttered the scribbled words from the crinkled page. He, too, could feel a dark, heavy energy burning through it as he placed the folded piece of paper into his pocket. "Kids, go home. Lock yourselves inside the safest room of your house. On this night, the barrier that protects the living from the dead is weakest. I'm not sure if anything on this page is even true, but we can't risk it. Not tonight." Mr. C. lowered the page and huddled the kids together. "Listen. If you fall asleep, you may be in danger of parasomnia pseudo-suicide. Get rid of any dangerous or sharp objects in the room you choose, and try to stay awake. I don't know of any way to track such a demon other than to study where it's already been." Thomas knew exactly what Mr. C. meant. He knew that the demon would most likely show up to finish killing Jack. "There's no sense in trying to predict where a predator might go without any trail or evidence. Just take extra precautions tonight. Stay safe until I can figure this out. I want to believe you're telling the truth about the things you saw in the hollow. I just need some time to process everything. I should've never told you that fucking story; I just need you safe. Now go!"

The kids stood nonplussed, motionless under the orange haze of the salissant parking garage. They knew they had to run, but fear has a way of cementing your feet to the ground when you least expect it.

"Thomas. Em. Max...Paige, you need to go." Mr. C. looked each of them in the eyes. This time he made an effort to speak softly in order to free them from the invisible binds of disquietude. "I need to be with my son now, and you need to go home. I'm sorry for the things my ancestor did, but I need you to trust me. Drive safe!" Mr. C. watched as Paige slowly nodded and retreated to the SUV. He turned to the others. Wide-eyed and worried, they reluctantly followed suit. "Stay in touch, kids; and remember, try to stay awake." He sighed as he watched the kids slowly drive away.

Emerlyn and Thomas both paused before going their separate ways. They locked eyes for a few moments but said nothing. Their body language said it all, each silently screaming for the other to stay. It was too harsh a reality for Emerlyn and Thomas to fully comprehend as they felt the fear of losing a mostly unspoken bond for eternity.

Mr. C. quickly made his way back to Jack's room. He quietly opened the door so as to not startle his wife who was sitting next to Jack and fiddling with the tv remote. "Sweetie, I know you're going to have a hard time with this, but there's something I need to tell you." Mr. C. nervously joined his wife in a cold, pleather chair near Jack's bed.

"Yes, Dear?" she replied in a worried tone.

"Look, I know you hate my stupid stories and conspiracies, but this is about our son," Mr. C. paused, leaning forward and placing his hand on hers.

"No, Philip. Not here. Not tonight. And most certainly, not now!" She withdrew her hand from his. "I don't want to hear it."

"I need you to hear me out." This time Mr. C.'s voice was deeper and more forceful. "The kids went to the hollow last night. I think it has something to do with Jack's incident."

"What on earth are you talking about? He was home when this happened! We saw it on video!" she pleaded.

"Just let me finish, Woman! They came across Holcomb's grave. Well, one thing led to another; and Jack had to pull Thomas out of the reverend's coffin. The kids told me that weird things started happening." Mr. C. paused for a moment as Jack twitched and groaned in the bed.

"It's nothing. He's been doing that for a while now. The doctor said it's normal to see involuntary movements and muttering," Mrs. C. interrupted his thoughts.

Mr. C. turned back to his wife. "Emerlyn said she saw Amelia."

"Are you seriously going to sit there and tell me you believe a scared child's ghost tales on Halloween? Are you out of your mind? She's processing a lot of emotional trauma right now. We are all going through exorbitant amounts of stress." His wife's voice was filled with hysteria.

"They said they caught her on camera. I think we did, too! The girl in the security footage. She fits their description of Amelia to a T." Mr. C. tried to calm himself, keeping an even tone in his voice. "Look at this." He pulled the grimoire page from his pocket. "Emerlyn found this in Amelia's cabin, today. It has to be from a larger book. The weird things that started after Jack removed Thomas from the grave, I think it has something to do with the thing described in this document. Look! It is even signed in the name Amelia Groeh! There haven't been any Groeh's in this town for a long time. There's no way the kids could have faked this document, and their descriptions of tunnels and passages in the hollow are eerily similar to some of the sketches I have in my secret collection." Mr. C. noticed a slight shift of attitude in his wife's eyes. "Thomas found my grandfather's grave in ruins. Why would anyone do that unless they knew about his involvement in the church's corruption? He wasn't a perfect man. He'd pushed for indulgences and was a practitioner of questionable religions, but who else would know this kind of thing? I have all of my grandfather's old journals locked away!" he paused and once again, turned his attention to Jack. "Do you think our son would do such a thing out of shame? What if he has something to do with this grimoire that the kids are talking about?"

"That's it! I've heard enough of your shit for one night!" Mrs. C. shot up from her chair. "I can't take anymore of your wild imagination. This all sounds like something orchestrated out of that crazy collection of books you have in the den. I need you to let go of all that hokey bullshit and be the man I married! I can't be around this superstitious version of you anymore. It's poisoned our son! It's poisoning our marriage!"

"Alice, where are you going? It's late." Mr C. stood up as his wife grabbed her keys and headed for the door.

"I need some air. I'm going for a drive. Call me if our son wakes up, Philip." Her words were cold and her compassion far removed, as she let the hospital door slowly close behind her.

Mr. C. looked down at his son, "Wake up, Jack. I need you to wake up, Son. It's not safe for you to be asleep."

MOCKOVIAK

Chapter 14

The enervate, yellow star retreated below the darkened horizon; but its rollicking rays scattered far and wide across the wild blue yonder, piercing the ocean of atmosphere above, creating a new diffusion of color palettes only a superlunary outlander could possibly envision. Thomas and Max cast flickering shadows across the charcoal-colored pavement as they passed the unsightly jack o'lanterns that lined their little bourgeois driveway. The crookedly carved, malformed faces stared with hauntingly watchful eyes that coruscated from the dancing candlelight. Suddenly, a single incandescent bulb turned on inside the living room. The two watched elegiacally through the window as they approached the front door. It was the only sign of life that Thomas and Max ever received from their uncaring, woebegone mother.

"I know this goes without saying," Thomas muttered to his brother, "but you know we can't tell Mom about any of this, right?"

"I know," Max whispered semi-mournfully. "Since dad left, she's been more of a ghost than Amelia. She's never sober enough to have a real conversation, anyway."

"I know, Max, but at least we have each other. You're all the family I'll ever need, even though you're annoying as fuck." Thomas giggled as he opened the front door and turned on the kitchen lights.

"Oh, I'm annoying? Whatever you say, El Capitán Douche Nozzle."

"Max, you have such a wonderful way with words." Thomas laughed as he held the door open for his brother. The slender shadow of their malnourished mother caught the corner of his eye as she sneakily returned to her room. "She never cared much for our half-witted humor." Thomas's desultory remark was not lost on Max.

"So what's the plan?" Max's inquiry was followed by a massive sigh as he watched the faint glow of the bedimming sun retreat to the other side of the world. He wished he could follow it and leave this hollow house behind. His brain was running off of fear and fumes. His angry, growling stomach reminded him that they hadn't eaten lunch; and apparently they'd missed supper, too.

"Well, judging by the God-awful sounds that your body is making, I'd say we should get you something to eat." Thomas pointed to the freezer. "I'm sure there are plenty of dino nuggets left."

"Oh my God! Dino nuggies!" Max exclaimed as he skipped enthusiastically towards the freezer door. "And tater tots! And also, extra crispy tendies!"

"After that, we just survive." Thomas forcefully swallowed the stubborn lump of terror that continued to linger in the back of his throat. He didn't want to admit it; but he was feeling tired, defeated, and losing focus. The incessant stress of the day had worn him down. "Contrary to popular opinion, the best way to survive a shit-hits-the-fan scenario is to hunker down and try to wait it out. Even Mr. C. told us to find a safe room for the night. It's not like we can run from it."

"Can we stay in your room?" Max asked as he read the cooking instructions on the back of the box of nuggets and the bag of tots. "I have ninja swords on my wall and that cool stun gun that I bought at that cheap Cajun market last year, so we definitely can't sleep in there. Oh! If we do bug out, we should go hide from the demons in Louisiana! We could buy combat shotguns! And we could hunker down in the Atchafalaya Basin! We can't go to Jersey, though. I hear there's a devil there already..."

"Yea, Max." Thomas interjected. "We can bunk in my room tonight, but you better shower first. Last time you slept in my room, it smelled like old fart for a whole week!" Max's unusual silence was a strong indicator that Thomas was telling the truth. "Also, I don't think using guns would do much against an invisible Dream Demon. Look how it turned out for Jack." Thomas's sanguine timbre abruptly degenerated into sadness as he reflected on the woes of the day.

"You're sounding kind of tired, Bro." Max tried his best to motivate Thomas with his legendary Coach Rick Vice impression, stringing together an endless sea of profanity and nonsensical inspirational quotes. However, his mind was already drifting to some other dimension. Thomas was a thinker, and the weight of the day had taken a serious toll on his mind and his body. He knew the rules. Find a safe place to shelter for the night and absolutely no sleeping. Unfortunately, he hadn't slept much the night before; and his eyes longed for rest, growing heavier and heavier with each passing minute.

As Max headed for the shower, he crept past his mother's darkened, idiosyncratic bedroom. An unusual, wooden beaded curtain hung in place of a conventional door. Max always did his best not to look through the dark, eerie gaps between the rattling beads. He feared what might linger just beyond the peculiar curtain. From time to time, he could hear a slight rustling behind the noisy portière. It always felt like something sinister was watching, waiting within the blackness. Maybe that's why his mother never turned on the lights. Maybe it wouldn't let her.

Thomas rubbed his full belly as he put the leftover tendies and tots back into the warm oven, covering them with a sheet of the loudest foil known to mankind. He winced at the harsh crackling sounds of the tinfoil as he pressed the corners around the warped baking tray and slowly closed the obnoxiously squeaky oven. He knew that Max would come back for more later. He always did.

Thomas made his way towards his bedroom, carefully tiptoeing past his mother's doorway. He too, feared that room. The zany curtain appeared to come alive at night. With every step forward, the floorboards seemed to scream in agony, each sorrowing bellow giving away his current location. Thomas's muscles were rigid as he fearfully anticipated any sudden movement of the obstreperous curtain of beads. He inched past the dark doorway, and suddenly it felt like someone was just behind him, watching. Thomas's curiosity and paranoia were overpowering. He turned around, squinting at the black bedroom. He craned his neck in a final attempt to uncover the identity of the mysterious entity that lurked within the room. There was nothing but silence.

Thomas exhaled loudly as he attempted to rid his body of anxiety. Suddenly, there was a direful rattling. The hair on his neck stood up and his eyes watered behind his crooked glasses. A short, thin shadow quickly emerged from the disquieting curtain. The sound seemed to rattle right through his bones.

"I'm leaving for work, Thomas."

"Mom?" Thomas's heart thumped so loudly that it almost interrupted his words.

"Who else would it be, Son?" The hollow voice answered back as the sickly silhouette trudged away in sadness.

The curtain continued to clatter, and the darkness seemed to ooze and pulsate between the gaps as each string of beads continued to swing behind the torpefied, phantom figure.

Thomas quickly retreated to the safety of his room, passing the steam that enveloped the cracks of the bathroom door. He heard his brother singing "The Final Countdown" in the shower. If Thomas didn't know any better, he'd think Max was completely oblivious to the fact that a demon was almost certainly haunting them on Halloween night.

Thomas swiftly shut the door behind him and readied his Bigfoot VR game. It was the only thing that ever brought his anxious mind any peace, but tonight was different. All of his fellow squatchers were out having fun on All Hallows Eve; and he was stuck at home, hiding from the threat of an inter-dimensional parasite. Without the lively banter of his on-line friends, Thomas found it extremely hard to keep his eyes open. The somnolent, foggy atmosphere of the Redwood forest magnified his exhaustion, but he was determined to get the job done.

An endless sea of sparkling stars blanketed the cobalt sky above, casting a pale glow of shimmering white light that washed over the massive sword ferns below. A narrowing path of crumbling grey soil and red fallen limbs lay before him, winding in and out of the colossal tree trunks, dodging the never-ending webwork of roots. A deep growl rumbled straight through his chest, and a series of unnatural whoops and screeching caterwauls followed thereafter. Thomas equipped his tranquilizer gun, donned his night vision goggles and headed out of base camp. Tonight, he'd try a more aggressive approach to hunting Bigfoot.

This was the new Halloween DLC. The terrain was tough, foreign, but oddly familiar. Part of the main path was lined with a plethora of menacing jack o'lanterns ranging in all shapes and sizes. The dancing orange flames licked the insides of the flickering eyes and scintillating mouths, emitting a soft glow that guided Thomas further into the hauntingly beautiful forest. Towering scarecrows with burlap-stitched faces and dingy, desolate peepers greeted him in the shadows as he rounded the first turn on the trail. It was hard to see, and his wild imagination began playing tricks on him. Thomas pulled the white phosphor night vision goggles over his dilated eyes, and the dark world around him was re-illuminated in an ocean of blue-green light.

The winding path that lay before him was unnervingly familiar, but the landscape made no sense. There were glowing orbs in the distance that nearly blinded him through the night vision device. Thomas could feel it in his gut. Something was amiss. He could hear low growls and grumbles coming from the direction of the levitating lights. Was it Bigfoot? Or was it something else entirely? Thomas's vivid imagination cycled through horrific images and endless paranormal possibilities. Thoughts of inter-dimensional travelers, aliens, skinwalkers, and UFO's flashed before his very eyes like an old film reel taken straight from an unacknowledged special access program. In a word, he was terrified to follow the Sasquatch snarls, fearful of encountering something even more terrifying.

He'd long since left the ominous scarecrows and disfigured pumpkins behind. The footpath was leading Thomas out of the forest, but he knew he was hot on Bigfoot's trail. The sounds grew louder as he carefully approached the glowing spheres of white light. It seemed the Sasquatch had wandered into a creepy neighborhood with old, rusted road signs and houses that had a haunted, eldritch look about them. The sinister vibes were accentuated by the low-lying fog that eerily crept across the barren lawns and empty streets. Still, it all seemed uncomfortably familiar. Thomas's eyes were fatigued from the blue-green hue of the night vision. He lifted the goggles away from his eyes, revealing the soft glow of the blemished moon above. The orbs were much dimmer to the naked eye and seemed to be distant security lights, indicating active residents. Thomas let out a heavy sigh. He did not want to follow any further, but the beast had to be stopped before it hurt someone.

His target was lightning fast. Thomas only caught quick, fragmented glimpses of the elusive creature in the darkness. It was as though Bigfoot was nothing more than a hollow silhouette dancing between the starlight and the safety of the next available shadow. That old familiar feeling of terrific terror began to crawl up the back of his neck and tiptoe across his scalp, but he was committed to finally cornering the cryptid. Thomas mimicked the creature's movements, strategically using the shadows as natural camouflage, staying low to the ground in order to prevent the possibility of casting a silhouette of his own. With those ancient techniques, he finally found himself on an empty street, mere feet away from Bigfoot. Thomas's hands shook, and his legs began to tremble. He could barely hold his tranquilizer gun as a feverish feeling and weakness spread throughout his body like a viral infection. It was his fight or flight mechanism in overdrive.

Slowly, the silhouetted cryptid creature turned towards Thomas, and for the very first time, he saw its eyes. They were glowing like the orbs he'd seen before, growing brighter and brighter with each passing moment. The massive shadow was rapidly approaching. Something wasn't right. Within seconds, the monster's glaring white eyes had grown several times larger than before, and they were still growing. They were so debilitatingly bright that Thomas had to squint and shelter his face with the shadow of his hand in order to see anything at all. For a split second, he felt like he was in one of those over-the-top alien abduction movies filmed in the backlots of Hollywood.

A loud screeching sound began echoing through the streets. Thomas knew this wasn't a sound that Bigfoot would ever make. The shrills pierced the cool autumn air and reverberated deep within his bones. Thomas's senses were completely overloaded. The blinding lights, the ear-splitting sounds, and the sudden adrenaline rush crippled him, cementing his legs to the ground. He couldn't move. Then, there was another sound. Is that a horn? His mind raced with thoughts. Finally, he mustered up enough willpower to move, but his fatigued, spaghetti legs buckled under the pressure. Thomas dropped to his knees. Then, there was nothing but black.

Crushed by a speeding truck in the middle of the street leading up to his house, Thomas's bleeding, battered body lay there on the ground, convulsing in the flickering orange candlelight of the jack o'lanterns that lined his driveway. His right elbow and left knee were bent in the wrong direction, snapping them completely out of place. Copious amounts of crimson-colored blood and yellowish body fluids gushed out of his body, pouring over the pavement, around the pumpkins, and into the grass. Thomas's left eye was dislodged. It dangled just outside of its bloody socket beneath his cracked glasses. His top lip was ripped away, and his front teeth had been ground across the blacktop until they were nothing more than tiny fractured nubs protruding from his exposed, bleeding gums. Parts of his shattered rib cage splintered through his pierced skin and bulged beneath his shredded clothing in pools of coagulating blood. The entire neighborhood heard the accident, but Max was the first to find his brother's mangled mess of a body. It was still twitching in the candlelight.

Chapter 15

On this evening, the undying twilight seemed unusually reluctant to give way to the inevitable darkness that approached. It clung to life the way Jack did in this awful, drab hospital bed. Mr. C. hoped that as one sun slowly gave way to the dark, his son would soon find the strength to rise from the relentless entrenchment of death that so impatiently salivated for his soul. He stared through the crooked creases in the blinds, louring into infinity, feeling so ephemeral and infinitesimal to the rest of the world. All the while, his entire world lay lifeless in bed. A single tear rolled down his face and landed on Jack's wrist near his hospital ID bracelet.

"Dad?" a crackling voice whispered in confusion.

"Son? Jack?" There was nothing but silence. "Talk to me Jack," Mr. C. 's tears multiplied into rivers as his only son, his sole seed slowly came back to life before his tired, red eyes.

"Dad, I'm thirsty."

"Yes, of course, Son. The nurse brought some ice chips for you." Mr. C. reached for the white styrofoam cup and plastic spoon, carefully placing tiny pieces of ice onto Jack's drying lips.

"Thank you, Dad." Jack coughed and winced at the sudden feeling of horrific pain emanating from his mutilated femur.

"You're lucky, ya know." Mr. C. examined his son's leg bandages. "Just missed your femoral artery. Doctor said you could have bled out in only a few minutes. Why'd you do it, Son?" Mr. C looked up from the bandages, wiping away his tears. "What'd you see?"

"Dad, everything is fuzzy. I can't remember. I thought I saw Paige, but then it wasn't her." Jack's voice was saturated with pain and disorientation. "Where's Mom? Is she here?"

"Your mother went out for some air. She couldn't have gone too far, but I need you to think, Son. Where's the book?" Mr. C.'s tone was both pleading and demanding. "I know you were up to no good. I mean, how could you desecrate your ancestor's tombstone? No matter his dodgy reputation, we must preserve history! If we destroy it, how can we ever learn from it?" This time, a sharp hint of anger seeped through his voice. "What did you do in the hollow? I need to know about everything! I need to know about the book." Mr. C. removed the wrinkled, leathery page from his pocket.

Jack's eyes strained to focus on the grisly imagery, seemingly inked in bodily fluids, front and back. "Dad, I don't know what you're talking about." He rubbed his eyes in an effort to correct his blurry vision. "All we did was take a picture."

"A picture? Of what?" Mr. C.'s voice teemed with a sense of impatience, but he could tell that Jack was telling the truth.

"Yea, just a picture. Thomas fell into a coffin, but I didn't desecrate any graves. I didn't even see any family headstones when I was there. It was dark." Jack grimaced as he shifted his injured leg in bed. "There was this horrible apparition that showed up on the photograph. We thought it might be Amelia."

"Where is it? Where's the photograph?" Mr. C. stared into his son's eyes with a stern, Rhadamanthine look of seriousness.

"It's on my phone," Jack replied as his hoarse voice cracked. "Where's my phone?"

"Your nightstand..." Mr. C. mumbled as he remembered Deputy Huey placing Jack's phone onto the nightstand. "So you're telling me that you had nothing to do with a grimoire or a spellbook of any kind?"

"Dad, I swear that I have no idea what you're talking about. All we did was walk around and take a photo in front of that old tree." Jack's mind was still slowly waking up. "Paige! How is she? We had a big fight after that thing showed up on my phone. It's all my fault, Dad. I shouldn't have dragged her to the hollow. I shouldn't have carved our names on that dumb tree."

"Carved your names, too? Listen. It's okay, Son. Paige has been here by your side all day. She loves you. I believe you've been honest with me, but I have some really bad news." Mr. C. gently grabbed his son's injured hand and looked him straight in the eyes. "I have to leave now, and you're coming with me."

"Wait, what?" Jack's leg was still throbbing from his slight movements.

"It's not safe. You're in danger. The thing on this page, the dybbuk, I believe it's after you. I can't take the risk of leaving you here. If you fall asleep, I fear it will come for you again." Mr. C. firmly grasped his son's wrist while supporting his back. "I need you with me." He carefully lifted Jack out of bed; a surge of intense twinges, aches, and pains crippled him as he groaned in agony.

"I can't do it, Dad. I can't go!" Jack cried out to his father.

"Yes, you can. You have to do this with me, Jack. I can't lose you, my son." Mr. C. tried to hide the tears in his voice. "I need to have a look at that photograph on your phone. I need to figure this thing out. We have to go, now. Don't do this for me. Do it for Paige. This Dream Demon could be after her, too."

Jack's fearful, teary eyes were suddenly filled with a fiery look of confidence and determination. It was his love for Paige that filled his mind, body, and soul with the strength to sit up in bed. He removed the intravenous drip from his hand and used his gown to stop the bleeding.

"Stay here for a minute while I find some gauze and a wheelchair." Mr. C. left the room and swiftly returned with the chair and bandaging. "Come on, Hotwheels," Mr. C. giggled with Jack through the pain of wrapping his hand and lifting him into the wheelchair. "Well, I don't know what looks worse, your leg or that beat up hand of yours. Looks like you had a few wounds on it before the IV."

"It's been a long weekend." Jack forced a grin as he looked up at his father.

"It ain't over yet, Son." Mr. C. faced Jack and leaned forward. "I need you to know that I love you."

"I know, Dad. I love you, too." Jack smiled as tears rolled down his face, each one finding its way across the creases and dimples of his cheeks. "Now, let's get the fuck outta here."

Mr. C. nodded and burst into laughter. "That's my boy." He stood up straight and grabbed the handles behind the wheelchair, pushing Jack out into the hallway. "Oh! Let me know when you need something for the pain. I may or may not have accidentally ventured into the pharmacy storage."

"Thanks, but I don't know what's more pained right now-my leg or my pride after wearing this stupid gown," Jack replied only half-jokingly.

Chapter 16

Paige sat in her driveway shell-shocked, shattered, and shaky as she drowned herself in the sorrowful melodies of the sad music that played over the radio. Her stunning beauty and habitually well-kept appearance was all but gone, hidden beneath the blank look of sadness and exhaustion daubed across the creases of her bone-weary face.

She sat staring through the filthy windshield of the SUV; her lifeless gaze happening upon the overpriced silk curtains and gaudy decor that lined the front of her house. It wasn't really her house anymore, not since she grew a pair of tits and an ass to grab. She might as well be propped up on the corner of the porch like the expensive Halloween decorations or more accurately, an oversold slut. Somewhere along the way, Paige had lost her parents' love to an unquenchable thirst for power and money. All their delusions of grandeur came with a cost, and her parents weren't the only ones expected to pay the price. She was no longer a daughter to love and protect but an attraction for creeps, an exhibit for peeping toms, a shiny little plaything for handsy, old men and women.

Even now, as Paige slowly trudged through the sparkling, orange lights and billowing grey clouds of artificial fog that hovered heavily around the front door, all the disgusting perversions that plagued the house were immensely overshadowed by the hellish nightmare she'd endured since the hollow. The traumatizing photograph, Mr. C's dire warnings, her friends' overwhelming tales of demonic entities, and thoughts of Jack and their unborn baby violently swirled around inside her enigmatic mind, smothering her fragmented heart with grief, fear, and anxiety. But none of that mattered now, not here, not in this house.

"Oh! Paige, you're a disgusting mess!" A tall, busty woman with long, dark hair and a slinky, slitted black dress rudely greeted her at the door.

It was the real Mistress of the Dark, her mother. "Paige, for God's sake! Don't let any of the guests see you like this! Go get cleaned up, and get dressed right now! You have less than an hour!" Her mother adjusted her fake breasts, smoothed out the lines in her designer dress, and gawked at Paige's unsatisfactory waistline. "Paige, you're getting a little pudgy. Maybe instead of riding around in Jack's truck all the time, you might consider jogging? And if you're not going to work on your thigh gap, please cover it up with something nice!"

"Mom, I don't know how you do it." Paige stared into her mother's black, soulless eyes. "You always manage to dig up every single insecurity that I have and throw them all in my face while smiling. I don't know where we went wrong, but there's no coming back from this, Mother." Paige's eyes filled with tears as she brushed past the contorted curtain of cobwebs that hung behind her mother and retreated to the safety of her room.

Paige stepped in front of the tall mirror and removed her clothing, revealing an hourglass shaped body and tiny baby bump. Her eyes gravitated towards the parts of her body that her mother described as flawed. She took a step forward, leaning into her own reflection while examining the lines and creases that sneakily snaked across her thin cheeks and nested in half-circles under her tired eyes. A long white strand of hair emerged from her head and dangled in front of her nose.

If pain is beauty, then why do I still feel so ugly? Paige thought to herself as she removed the grey. It was all becoming so nauseating. The facade of perfection always fades behind closed doors. She continued to run her fingers through her long brunette bangs, weeding out the recalcitrant white and grey stragglers.

She stepped into the scalding shower, the swirling vapor glistened around her reddening, pale skin; each painful drop of hot water seemed to temporarily ease her emotional torment. Paige took a long, deep breath, inhaling large clouds of steam as she fell to her knees. She pushed her wet hair back behind her head and buried her face in her palms. Whether it was the fear of losing Jack, the dread of being fondled at this aristocratic sex party, the crushing weight of her insecurities, or the searing pain from the curtain of boiling water that overtook her body, Paige couldn't help but sob. She bit the inner part of her thumb and screamed into her hands.

Her knees dug into the shower drain as she shifted her weight forward and continued to cry.

"Why, God? Why me?" she whispered through hysterical whimpers.

Paige reluctantly pulled herself together for one last show; she'd never do this again. She dried herself, applied a generous amount of pumpkin body butter to her skin, styled her hair, and dropped the wet towel onto the floor while reaching for the pre-approved costume. It was a skimpy blue-and-white gingham pinafore dress, complete with pigtails and ruby red heels. There really is no place like home. She thought as a few more tears rolled down her rosy cheeks.

"Mother, you might actually be the most wicked witch on the planet."

There was a startlingly harsh knock on the door. "Paige, it's almost time for the ceremonial toast! Get your ass out here!" Her father, seemingly oblivious to it all, demanded her presence. His voice muffled behind the closed door. "Your mother will kill both of us if you fuck this up!"

The bitter words that left her father's lips festered in a vat of nervousness, buried deep in the pit of Paige's soured stomach. There were a lot of reputations riding on the success of the night's under-the-table deals and bargains. She just wished she wasn't a part of it. As Paige put on the dress, another wave of nausea rushed over her. She raced to the bathroom sink, puking up yellow and green bile. Is it the baby or just the fact that my life is falling apart? Paige thought as she rinsed her mouth and cleaned the sink, taking one last miserable look in the mirror. Her eyes were still sad, her smile, fake. No one would notice. No one would care enough to notice. Jack was in the hospital; and no one cared enough to notice that, either. All that mattered was that her figure was attractive enough to ogle from a distance.

Paige reluctantly unlocked her bedroom door and took the first step into the hallway. She could already hear her parents' intoxicated laughter and guests chattering in the dining area. An old recording of "Danse Macabre" was playing on a record from somewhere inside the ever-thickening fog and twinkling pumpkin lights. Vibrant hues of blood red and ultraviolet lights lined the baseboards and corners of every room, making it hard to see the wooden floor lurking beneath the bright blanket of colorful clouds that swirled around her red heels.

Suddenly, various masked silhouettes of men and women seemed to manifest from the darkness to greet her.

"Hello there, Miss Paige. Might I say, you look ravishing!" a slightly familiar masculine voice called to her as his long finger rubbed against the outline of her jaw, stopping just below her lips.

"Miss Paige, a pleasure as always," a feminine voice whispered intimately into her ear as a different hand caressed her shoulder.

"Paige!" her mother called from the head of a long, rosewood dining table at the far end of the house. The room was more isolated and illuminated only by candlelight, enhancing the seemingly Luciferian vibes that filled the house. It was more like devil worship than a party. "Let's not keep the guests waiting any longer. Shall we?" She gestured in an Elvira-esque manner towards a golden chalice meant for Paige. It was the only cup not yet filled. As part of a bargain with her father, Paige convinced him to allow her to abstain from drinking any alcohol at the party, including the ceremonial wine. "Paige, darling. I don't know what you plan on pouring into that cup, but I suggest you make it quick," her mother whispered aggressively into her ear. "The guests are ready to mingle."

Paige reached for a secret stash of sparkling grape juice hidden next to the wine. She quickly opened the bottle, poured the naturally carbonated drink into her chalice, and smiled at her mother. It was a smile, but for all intents and purposes it was also a fuck you.

"Attention!" The drunken chitter-chatter ceased as her mother raised her cup with one hand and flipped through an old, leathery book with the other.

Paige hadn't noticed the book until now, but it looked a lot like the grimoire her friends warned about. Her heart started pounding inside her head as a dark fountain of anxiety poured over her soul. The pages were scribbled in different handwritings and riddled with crude sketches of perverse rituals.

Could it really be the spellbook? Paige's thoughts were racing; her eyes were shifting back and forth between the book and her mother's nauseatingly theatrical expressions.

"We dare trek where even Heaven's mightiest angels do not! Fools, they call us," Paige's mother continued. "On this night, when the veil is thin, we welcome friends of new and friends of old back into the fold. What happens here, within our circle of trust, cannot and will not leave our circle of trust. Together, we can transcend society's fallacy of limitation, tipping the scales of fortune in our favor. There are no fools here." Shadows danced across the table, skewing the symmetry of painted faces and masked men.

Paige's father, dressed as Vlad the Impaler, raised his golden cup high in the air. The costumed guests mimicked the vampire's motions, and Paige did, too. "Under this full moon, we drink to fill our unfettered, ataraxic souls with sweet serenity and drink to sewing our most precious seeds with success!"

Her father and mother turned to each other, allowing the rims of their cups to touch before drinking. Paige turned to her side and touched her chalice to that of a gentleman that resembled the Phantom of the Opera. Only part of his face was visible, but she could tell he was grinning. As they drank, their eyes met; and for a moment, it was almost charming.

After the opening ceremony, the crowded table quickly dispersed throughout the entirety of the house. Some of the witches retreated to their cauldrons in the kitchen, where they whipped up cocktails laced with anything and everything under the moon. A Lurch look-alike sat at a bench playing the harpsichord while a gothic couple lustfully teased and toyed with each other. Paige sat amidst the fog with her pigtails and little pinafore dress, attempting to avoid the busiest parts of the party and to stay far away from that spellbook. She placed her drink down on the coffee table behind her and continued to people-watch. Some of the other parents had their young daughters with them. It was easiest to spot the young girls in their costumes, because none were allowed to wear much clothing at all. The skimpier, the better. Walking, talking, future trophy wives is all they were. In the eyes of her parents, Paige was no different.

Suddenly, she felt the light nudge of a hand on the small of her back. Paige's body tightened, and she jolted forward from the touch.

"I didn't mean to frighten you." The masked figure's voice was soft and comforting.

"Oh, it's you again! Mr. Phantom, right?"

"Well, I'm gonna level with you. I picked this costume up on the way here, and I know nothing about Halloween parties. Mr. Phantom works, I suppose." The man grinned behind the mask. "So is this how you always dress? Or are you some kind of character?"

"Well, it's my turn to level with you. I dress this way every single day. I'm totally just dressed as Paige right now. Who else would I be?" Paige raised an eyebrow and smirked.

"I don't know. It was hard to recognize you without your little dog, too."

"Oh, you're just full of jokes tonight, Mr. Phantom. It's been a real pleasure, but I'm going to go find my dad, now. I don't plan on sticking around this place for very long."

"Wait, before you go..." The mysterious man handed Paige her chalice of sparkling juice. "How about one last toast?"

"A toast to what, exactly?" Paige took her cup.

"How about a toast to making new friends?" He raised his glass.

"Fine. To new friends." Paige tapped his glass and drank the last of her drink. "Well, looks like I'm all out. No more toasting for me. I was getting a little tired of holding this giant cup, anyway."

"Is that why you had it on the coffee table?" The tone of the phantom's voice became slightly more sinister.

"Yea, I guess so..." Her mouth went numb, and Paige began slurring her words. She was feeling disoriented and horror-stricken. Her first instinct was to retreat to the safety of her bedroom. Paige turned from the masked man, dropping her cup into the fog. She stumbled and swayed her way through the hall, at last reaching the door to her room.

Paige's senses were bombarded with flashing lights, loud music, and intoxicated laughter behind her. She tried to close the door, but fell face-first onto her bed. Suddenly, her phone began to buzz.

"Max?" She read through her blurry vision. "What the hell?" She pressed ignore on the phone and silenced it. "I don't have time for your shit right now, Max," she drunkenly whispered to herself as she finally managed to roll onto her back. Her eyes were even blurrier than before, and she squinted with all her might to see who was standing at the foot of her bed. "Jack? Is that you?" Paige whispered as her heavy eyes began to close.

She felt someone force himself under her dress, ripping her panties to the side. She limply kicked and crawled backwards, digging her ruby heels into the white sheets. It was a rough man's touch. His movements were so unfamiliar, his body so foreign.

It couldn't be Jack. Her inebriated mind reasoned.

She strained one last time to focus as the rhythm of his warm breath began to match her own. Through her foggy eyes, all Paige could see was the masked phantom forcibly thrusting atop her numbing body. She felt him sinking his teeth into the side of her neck as he pulled at her hair, coercing her to comply. Her rolling eyes caught a quick glimpse of her mother slowly closing the bedroom door and walking away. The drugged drink, the confusion, the excitement, and the rough nature of it all were absolutely, uncontainably orgasmic; and she reluctantly embraced it. That uncontrollable fact filled her broken heart with both ecstasy and shame as she came three times and bled all over the sheets. She felt a few more forceful, sharp thrusts deep inside her stomach; and then she blacked out in puddles of her own cum and blood.

Chapter 17

Emerlyn fought to keep her spalling thoughts together as she frantically closed the front door, locking the deadbolt behind her; lest there be a creeping, crippling ghoul nipping at her heels, lubriciously reaching for her Achilles' tendons. That interminable fear flowed through her veins and fluttered just behind her ears like little wings of an agitated cockroach noisily nesting within the wavy locks of her hair. A spine-tingling string of bifurcating chills ensued shortly thereafter. She'd scolded herself in the past for being overly paranoid, but this time her fear was anything but unreasonable or unjustified. Of course the house was dark, amplifying the dreadful pseudo-psychosis that continued to terrorize her mind. She could see orange and blue-white light flickering across the kitchen walls, shimmering over the tiled floor; her eyes watered. There were screams filled with agony and despair echoing throughout the house. Emerlyn crept into the kitchen, hesitantly peeking around the corner. A nervous nausea bled into her gut as she squinted her eyes, focusing on the silhouettes before her. An unintentional sigh of relief bellowed from deep within her chest as she identified her parents in the living room. They were cuddled on the sofa watching a horror movie marathon.

"Oh, Em! You're home! You nearly scared us half to death!" her mother exclaimed from the couch.

"Sorry, Mom! It's just been a rough day." Emerlyn hung her head as she walked briskly in front of the tv, recognizing the film at the corner of her eye. "*The Blob*?"

"The one and only," her mother replied with a snarky smile.

"How's Jack doing?" her father inquired. "Is he gonna pull through?"

"As well as he can be, I guess. He's been sleeping since the incident." Emerlyn shrugged her reply as she approached the hallway to her room.

Her syllables were shaky, and her voice was nervous. She didn't want her parents asking too many questions because they wouldn't like her answers. They wouldn't believe any of it. They'd blame it on an overactive imagination or some form of cognitive dissonance. Emerlyn took a deep breath and steadied her words. "Thanks for asking, Dad."

"How about we all go down to the hospital together? We can go first thing in the morning." Her father smiled and pulled her mother in closer, snuggling in a warm embrace.

"Yea, Dad. That'd be great," Emerlyn called back as she entered her bedroom. She didn't know if there'd even be a tomorrow, and that worry was markedly reflected in the tremulous timbre of her crepitating callback. All of her attention was on here and now. She was still doubtful any of her friends would survive the night.

Emerlyn reached for the crucifix around her neck and dropped to her knees. She whimpered quietly while looking up at her bedroom ceiling. Her gaze saw through it, mindfully staring into the heavens, hoping that the heavens were looking back at her. If she were being completely honest, though, part of her feared what kinds of cosmic horrors might actually take notice of her. She had no idea what was really out there. Not anymore. After all, she'd seen more darkness than light as of late.

"Are you there? I mean, are you really there?" she whispered as her lips touched the cross. "Is your name really Christ? Or are we Christians just living as slaves in a complete, fucking fabrication?" Emerlyn spoke frankly and choked on the last bit of her words as panic swelled in her breast and tears fell from her face. If there was no God, then she was truly alone in this fight. There'd be no help from her mother or father. That thought terrified Emerlyn down to her very core. "Did we get it all wrong? I need you to talk to me, God. Just this once. Please! I feel so alone!" She waited, staring up at the ceiling, the cross to her lips. She knelt patiently, quietly, pleadingly. She needed to hear a voice, something real. There was no reply, only dead air, only silence. That godless, empty atmosphere was quickly filled with the terrifying realization that evil was tangibly, factually real; and it was coming for her. In a cruel twist of fate, it was coming to get her in the exact same way that it had come for her grandmother, and there was nothing that she could do about it.

Emerlyn rose from her knees, wiping away her tears with one hand while the other still cradled the cross. For a brief moment, she considered clinging to hope; but that was no longer possible. It was no longer a viable option. She'd held onto that indefatigable hope so hard, for so long, that it had crippled her grip on reality and severed her spiritual sensibility. Emerlyn had grown tired of this mindless, insouciant, blind faith. She'd grown weary of not being able to read the writing on the wall. The only person that ever kept her grounded was Thomas. If it were not for his friendship, she might still be wandering aimlessly through life without questioning anything. She might feel that familiar false sense of security that she'd so often turned to in trying times. Tonight, she knew her prayers had fallen on deaf ears. She could feel it in the pit of her aching stomach, and Thomas always encouraged her to listen to her gut instinct.

"I should call him," Emerlyn whispered quietly as she stared at Thomas's contact photo. She smiled for a moment, recalling the bat encounter in the cabin. Desmodontinae? Who on Earth calls animals by their scientific names? Despite the horrors they'd encountered, Emerlyn couldn't help but giggle. "Yea, I should call him. But first, a shower."

She gathered her pajamas and proceeded down the dreaded hallway to her bathroom. She quickened her pace and diverted her eyes from that room at the end of the hall, fearful of what extra-dimensional beings might still be watching and waiting. Emerlyn swiftly entered the bathroom, flipped on the lights, and locked the door in double-quick time. She leaned forward with one hand high upon the door, the other lingering on the lock as she struggled to calm herself. She hung her head low, fighting to catch her breath. It was an irrefutable fact that Emerlyn was in the midst of a total breakdown. Perhaps she had just grown tired of constantly racing from one locked door to the next. Whatever the cause, it was obvious that she had reached her limit.

Emerlyn turned to the mirror above the sink. She removed her shirt and stared as her shaking, shivering hand slowly lifted the crucifix from her chest.

"I'm done, God. I just can't carry this anymore." Emerlyn muttered the words that she thought she'd never say, but it was the unfortunate truth.

Immaterial as it may seem to those around her, she felt her soul drying up, dying as it shriveled and withered away from spiritual neglect. She'd lost the last dwindling, dying ember of her unfrequented, disconsolate heart. As she somberly removed the cross, the rope pulled through her dark hair like a dredge, digging up the dead thoughts and putrid prayers she once held inside her moribund mind. She was no longer anchored to the stars, no longer tethered to the heavens.

Emerlyn peered into her tarnished reflection, looking into her own insensate, blue eyes. Much to her surprise, she stopped crying. There were no more tears left to shed, no more feelings left to feel. She clasped the cross one last time, held it to her heart, and then dispassionately dropped it into the trash can.

Turning from her apathetic, unbecoming reflection, she began to draw a bath. Still, in the corner of her eye, she thought she saw someone else in the mirror. "No, no, no. This is not happening again," she repeated under her breath. It happened before, but this was different. The other reflection seemed to unconsciously separate itself from her own, twisting and contorting into view, spasming and convulsing into apoplexy. "Eyes straight ahead on the bath. Don't give it any attention," Emerlyn scolded herself.

She could see the perverse astral projection peeling away in her peripheral vision. Maybe it was another trick of the mind, but she knew better. She'd always seen things. No matter how hard her father whipped her or how much her mother punished her, Emerlyn had always walked with the living and the dead. No amount of damnations, holy water, or scornful remarks could ever change that fact. All her life, it was de rigueur for her to look the part and act the part of an average, obedient Christian.

"No more lies. No more brainwashing," Emerlyn sighed.

She closed her eyes, squeezing them tightly as she lay back in the tub of warm water. Like long, slender tentacles of a magnapinna squid, her jet black hair branched out in all directions, curiously feeling, floating over and around her submerged, bubbling face. She exhaled slowly to keep the ever-encroaching water from filling up her lungs. It felt like bathing in a vat of blood, and inside her tormented mind, it looked a lot like La Resurrezione.

As Emerlyn slowly ascended to the water's surface, the black web of hair seemed to pull her back down to Hell. Each tentacle reluctantly unbound itself from Emerlyn's body as her chest burned to breathe new breath. She rose towards the surface and gasped for fresh air in the Garden of Gethsemane. Again, Emerlyn's mind was playing devilish tricks on her. Hallucinations or revelations? She couldn't decide. Either way, they were intensifying.

It had been days since she took the mind-altering medication she'd been force-fed for so many years. It had been weeks since she last stepped foot in the culty, community church. The truth was, Emerlyn was just empty. In spite of all the pills and all the prayers, she was still so eminently empty. She had been forced to deny a part of herself that was very real, painfully real. After all, she did take after her grandmother.

Dad got lucky.

Seems it skipped a generation, she thought as she washed away the remaining filth from her body and reached for a fresh towel.

"Em, won't you join us for a movie and hot chocolate?" Emerlyn's father called from the couch as she briskly exited the bathroom in a fresh pair of pajamas. "I promise, I didn't let your mother contaminate the recipe with any of that awful mint flavoring!" he added half-jokingly, winking at his wife.

"Yea sure, but only if you promise there's absolutely no mint in my hot chocolate!" Emerlyn called back from the hallway, hoping to earn participatory points with her parents by playing along with the dumb joke.

"Scout's honor!" her father replied teasingly.

Emerlyn's heart sank six feet under as she was reminded of Max and Thomas playfully bickering at one another in the hollow. Thomas really was a stereotypical boy scout, and Max would never let him forget it. Thinking of Thomas always made her heart feel kind of funny. She just hadn't really noticed it until today. Perhaps, it was the fear of losing him that suddenly made his presence seem more significant.

I really should call him, Emerlyn thought quietly to herself as she reluctantly approached the calls of her mother and father.

She had no choice but to join them for a while. If she retreated to her room to call Thomas, they would surely follow, prying as they did. She, Paige, and Jack were the oldest of the group at eighteen; but oh, how drastically different they were treated by their parents. She sighed internally. Emerlyn knew her parents loved her, but their love was sometimes suffocating to say the least.

"So what's up next on the Halloween playlist?" Emerlyn asked as she sat next to her father, carefully sipping hot chocolate. "Um, there's a disturbing lack of mini marshmallows in my cup!" she exclaimed, eyeing her mother with half a grin.

"Don't look at me Em," her mother retorted. "Your dad hogged all the marshmallows!"

"Well, ladies, all this talk of marshmallows has me thinking of the perfect movie!" Emerlyn's father grinned as he sipped from his oversized cup.

"I assume Mr. Stay Puft is involved in this production?" Emerlyn semi-enthusiastically inquired.

"*Ghostbusters* it is!" her father replied with a smile. His kind enthusiasm was genuine, but there was something else on his mind, something slightly sinister behind his grin. He was never any good at keeping secrets, and Emerlyn knew it wouldn't be long before he said what he was really thinking. "Em, you know I love you, right?" His voice and attitude shifted to a more serious tone as he removed something with an old familiar rattle from his pocket. The muffled sound of capsules tapping and tumbling against plastic filled the palm of his hand.

"Dad?" Emerlyn stared at the bottom of her empty cup as she wiped her numbing lips with a napkin. "What did you do?" Her eyes widened with fear.

"Your mother and I know you haven't been taking your medicine." Her father's complexion grew pale and cold as his body language became more rigid and authoritative. "I knew it the minute I saw you standing at your grandmother's door. You had that look in your eyes, again. You're covered in scrapes and bruises after ghosthunting with your friends," her father paused and sighed. "Ghosts aren't real, Em."

"Mom. Dad. What did you do to my drink?" Emerlyn began to panic. Her hands trembled as she placed the empty cup onto the coffee table.

"We did what we had to do, Baby Girl." Emerlyn's father held open his hand, revealing a new, stronger bottle of her prescribed medication. "We called your doctor today and told him you just misplaced your meds."

"Em, what you're seeing, it isn't really there," her mother interjected. "You're just sick, remember? This will help you relax, and you can just sit here with your father and me. We'll all have a nice Halloween together."

As the sedation set in, Emerlyn's vision began to blur. She could barely see straight, and there was an awful ringing in her ears. Or was it the phone? Emerlyn tried to read the caller ID on the bright phone screen, but her eyes couldn't seem to focus.

"It's okay Em. It's just Max calling. Whatever it is, I'm sure it can wait until the morning. We can all go visit Jack, together." Emerlyn's father took the phone from her hands and muted it, placing it face down on the couch.

Chapter 18

The seemingly undying, amber luminosity of October's endmost sunset finally gave way to the cold glow of the haunting, Halloween moon. It was a ceaseless combat over the heavens whereby the star eventually grew tired, only to temporarily retreat from the unsightly cicatrices of the cratered, stouthearted satellite. It was a constant reminder to Mr. C. that victory by attrition is still victory, and loss is still loss. He could not let his only son grow weary and fall, not to sleep and not to his certain death. His nervous eyes glanced back and forth between the double-yellow lines on the winding road and the ghostly reflections in the shimmering rearview mirror, half expecting to see a sadistic, concupiscent succubus salivating for his son's soul. Instead, he saw tired, tetchy parents chaperoning hyper, sugar-craving trick-or-treaters that hopped and skipped around the spooky neighborhood corn mazes.

"Here. Take this, Jack." Mr. C. removed a pain pill from the bottle he'd commandeered from the pharmacy and proceeded to break it in half. "Take it with the entire bottle of water that I have stored in the console. If you need the other half, don't hesitate to take it. But make sure you stay hydrated, lest you get a nasty little headache."

"Won't it make me sleepy?" Jack asked as he took one of the halves from his father's calloused hand and examined it.

"Thankfully, no. This should only give you a little buzz and perhaps keep the pain at bay," Mr. C. chuckled as he placed the vehicle in park. "We're here, Son."

Jack looked up from the powdery, white pill in his hand and saw his house through the grit of the dusty windshield. He was only away for a day, but the pain made it feel more like a lifetime.

"I'm going to retrieve your phone so we can have a look at that picture,"

Mr. C. continued. "I need to compare it to the girl I captured on the security footage. I want to see if that thing from the hollow really followed you home. I just need some help processing all of this." Mr. C. fondled the grimoire page in his pocket, still questioning its validity but heeding its warnings.

"Wait. Security footage?" Jack raised an eyebrow in confusion.

"Yea, don't worry. You're not in any trouble. I've had motion cameras around the house for years." Mr. C. turned and winked at his son. "Every time you snuck out or came home past your curfew, I knew about it. But you weren't a troublemaker, so I left you alone." Mr. C. leaned over and put his hand on Jack's shoulder. "You're a young man. You make your own decisions. The cameras are just here for security purposes. I always trusted you to come home safe."

"I feel so freakin' dumb. I can't believe I never noticed! I guess I let you down this time. I came home, but I wasn't exactly safe." Jack shook his head in embarrassment as he took the pain medicine and downed the entire bottle of water. "I'm going to need to pee soon, ya know?" Jack cracked a small smile as he showed his father the empty bottle. "And I'm going to need some legit clothes. I can't stay in this god-awful gown, Dad!"

"When you're right, you're right. I guess we're both getting down. Let me get your chair out of the back for you, Hotwheels." Mr. C. giggled as he opened the door.

"Again with the same wheelchair joke? Wow, I feel so loved." Jack closed his eyes and winced as he opened the passenger door and slowly shifted his injured leg in the seat, readying himself to transition to the chair. "Handicapable, Dad! Not handicapped!" Jack retorted in seemingly good spirits. "Also, I think I need some food. My stomach is so empty."

"Between you and that noisy stomach of yours, I don't know who groans more."

Mr. C. carefully, but speedily, positioned his son's legs and feet onto the shimmery footplates of the chair and wheeled him underneath the pale glow of the full moon. Jack couldn't help but look up and wonder if Paige was looking at it, too. She loved the moon, and he loved her to the moon and back.

"It's going to be a bit bumpy without a ramp at the door, so hold tight while I spin you around and pull you backwards," Mr. C. said, interrupting Jack's sentimental thoughts.

"Awe, geeze. I was hoping to at least pop a wheelie over the ledge." Jack's words were already slightly slurred from the medicine.

"Maybe next time I'll let you pop a wheelie, Hotrod," Mr. C. replied, rolling his eyes. "You believe in the Hollow Moon hypothesis, Jack?"

"Um, no...I don't believe it's an artificial satellite, Dad. I swear, sometimes I think Thomas is your real son. You talk about the craziest shit!"

"Don't knock the theory of a hollow moon until you research it. It's interesting.' Mr. C.'s thoughts drifted as his attention shifted back to the front door. He peeked in through the dark window, quietly turning the key inside the deadbolt. "Something isn't right, Son."

A mess of dark silhouettes lay disarranged across the floor. Mr. C. gestured towards Jack to stay quiet and slowly opened the door, his 10mm pistol drawn at the "compressed ready" position. He carefully made his way to the master light switch, quickly turning on every light in the house. His eyes strained to adjust to the bright lights, quickly shifting back and forth. He examined every nook and cranny of his personal armory, the library, and den to his left. Then, he cleared the kitchen and dining room to his right. There were books and trinkets all over the floor. Mr. C. did a quick shoulder check and turned to Jack.

"Deputy Huey didn't take your revolver for evidence, so I cleaned it up for you. She's loaded. Are you sober enough to handle it?" Mr. C. whispered as he motioned towards a cubbyhole near his gun cabinets.

"Yea, Dad. I'm good." Jack's eyes watered at the sight of the shiny, stainless barrel, sending a searing shock of pain straight through his bandaged leg.

His mind lit up like the Fourth of July; flashes of that putrid, inhumane face with those rotten, needle-like teeth flickered throughout his fragmented thoughts, overloading his fragile senses. That crippled, creeping creature crawled across his lap and laughed in twisted perversions of polyphonic overtones previously unheard by man. An endless supply of black goop of some sort seemed to ooze from every orifice of the maggot ridden monster, both seen and otherwise. Jack gagged at the thought of it all and instantly became nauseous. His bandaged hand trembled as he grasped the cold gun, the instrument of his mutilation.

"Watch my back. Keep an eye on the front door and the dining room," Mr. C. said as he walked through the den area, approaching the uninspected hallway from a narrow angle and mitigating his exposure.

It was the second time in one day that he felt violated, unsafe in his own home. The fear of a ghostly intruder burned through his veins, wriggled and writhed across his skin, and chilled him to the marrow. He took a deep breath and looked over at Jack one more time. He was doing his best to guard the open door and the front of the house from his wheelchair. Mr. C. slowly sliced the hallway with his muzzle at the "low ready" position, advancing to forty-five degrees and finally, snapping to a ninety. He stared intently down to the end of the hall, ready to blast anything that moved to high hell, but there was nothing.

"Are you sure you're not being paranoid?" Jack asked, his hands still trembling around the gun as he placed it gently onto his lap. "Couldn't it have been an earthquake or something?"

"Maybe," Mr. C. sighed, reholstering his weapon. "I need to check the damn security cameras, again. The thing we caught on video - it crawled through your bedroom window just minutes after we rushed you to the hospital. There's no video evidence of it leaving. I guess that still bothers me. I mean, it really bothers me. And all this? I don't know what to make of it."

Mr. C.'s thoughts were interrupted by a sudden burst of red and blue lights flickering and swirling behind Jack. A large-framed figure walked up to the open door, each step landing with the heavy thud of a boot and the distinct clanking of cuffs and keys on a leather gun belt.

"Sheriff Stone." Jack turned his chair facing the doorway, taking extra care to keep his hands away from the gun on his lap.

"Jack, haven't you had enough of that old revolver? I hear that's the one that landed you in a wheelchair in the first place." The sheriff shook his head in disapproval, an exasperated expression affixed upon his wrinkled face.

"Sheriff, to what do we owe the pleasure?" Mr. C. squinted, staring across the room at the towering man. "Aren't we Deputy Huey's little pet project? Did he shit his pants from all the Halloween spooks? Tell him

I'm working on a thin brown line patch for his vest. I'll send it over when I'm done."

"You mind your tone when talking about a dead man, Mr. Carter." The sheriff grimaced at Jack and his father.

"A dead man?" Mr. C. inquired as the color drained from his face, leaving him as pale as the corpse he imagined in his head.

"That's right, Philip, and it all has something to do with you and your son. I'm sure of it."

"Now, you better watch your tone in my house, Stone." Mr. C. walked towards the door, placing himself between the sheriff and his son. "You're an elected official, not some damn royalty."

"Why do you think it has something to do with us, Sheriff?" Jack interrupted, wheeling himself around his father. A look of anger and sadness was painted across Stone's grey eyes.

"Because it appears Deputy Huey took his own life. Now, I've known the kid since he was in diapers. This is completely out of his character!" A tear fell from his eyes, nestling itself between the cavernous wrinkles that plagued his thin cheekbones. "I hear that's the same thing people are saying about you, Jack. Completely out of your character as well, right?" Sheriff Stone stooped down so that he was eye to eye with Jack. "I know you are no stranger to that firearm in your lap, and you've got no obvious reason to harm yourself or anyone else, for that matter. So, please, tell me what the fuck is going on here."

"You wouldn't believe me if I told you," Mr. C. interjected. His voice was distant and slightly aloof. "I wouldn't believe me."

"Try me! A day ago I would've written you and your son off as meshuga, certifiable, or batshit crazy; but I've read Huey's report. I've seen the tapes." Stone leaned forward and tilted his large brimmed hat away from his line of sight, peeking around the doorway. "And I can see the mess about your house; quite uncommon for the neatest property on the block. Mr. Carter, the way I found Huey. . .It's inhuman to do things like that to yourself." That word, inhuman, stung Jack's ears and pained his battered leg.

"How exactly did you find him, Sheriff?" Mr. C.'s tone was still remote but somewhat sinister.

"Huey's father is a local farmer. You're familiar with the county corn mazes, I assume?" Sheriff Stone took a deep breath and looked away for a moment in a failed attempt to hide the tears that had stubbornly accumulated under his heavy eyes. "He must've fallen asleep on the property during the last few minutes of his shift. It's just east of here. About an hour later, it seems he stumbled out of his cruiser. The police dash cam auto-activated as he walked towards the crop duster plane near the hanger and the old barn. He appeared to be talking to someone or something just off camera. The footage becomes heavily distorted after that." The sheriff eyed Mr. C. and his son. "It was similar to the way your boy talked to a mysterious figure that seemed to interfere with your surveillance equipment." Mr. C. nodded. "If it weren't for the flames and billowing smoke acting like some sort of macabre signal fire, it might have taken us days to locate him. Huey's father and I found him beheaded and mangled into oblivion. Most of his body was found in chunks of bloody meat littered with shards of broken bone, strings of white and yellowish sinew, and pieces of bloodstained, shredded clothing. Bile, blood, and every other fluid you can imagine still covers the cold ground out there. His left leg and thigh were stubborn enough to stay connected to his torso, though, only by the tiniest bit of stringy flesh. I'm no doctor, but I'm pretty positive I had to wash splattered pieces of Huey's brain from the windshield of his cruiser. It resembled clumps of misshapen, wet noodles in size and texture. I can only hope he died quickly from the initial brunt of that horrifyingly crude decapitation. My guess, he must've walked into the spinning blades headfirst, on account of all the lumps of linguine. Hell, I don't know if we'll ever recover all the bits of his body. He, apparently, took it upon himself to get into the cockpit of that damned crop duster plane, start the engine, and then...He walked right into the blades of the propeller. Some shattered into lethally sharpened projectiles. Others were just bent all out of whack."

"Oh my God!" Jack put his bandaged hand over his mouth and shivered in his hospital gown.

"I assure you, God had nothing to do with this, Son," Sheriff Stone replied as he choked on the last of his words. "That sound like normal behavior to you, Mr. Carter? Did Huey just wake up this morning with the intention of throwing himself into a man-sized meat grinder? Or did something leave your house with my deputy? Something follow him to that cornfield, Mr. Carter? I know your family's history of devilish dealings and obsessions with unnatural things."

"I'm sorry, Sheriff. I really am, but I don't know what you want from us. I'm afraid we don't know much more than you do. We caught someone on tape breaking and entering just minutes after my son's incident, but we don't have much more than that." Mr. C.'s voice was still as cold as before. "Sure, the figure looked wounded and rather disturbing, but it's Halloween. It's getting harder and harder to tell what the hell is real anymore! In case you haven't noticed, it looks like someone broke into our home, again."

"Yea, it sure looks that way. Doesn't it?" Stone's bitterness showed through his furrowed brow and crinkled nose. "So you're not gonna help me, Philip? You're not gonna tell me there's a logical explanation for why my best deputy tragically died just hours after leaving your house?"

"I don't see how I can, Stone." Mr. C. motioned for Jack to get out of the doorway. "Now, if you don't mind, we have some cleaning up to do."

"Not as much cleaning up as Huey's father. If you're not careful, you'll have a much bigger mess on your hands, Mr. Carter. If you find yourself in a position to help, don't do it for me. Do it for your son." The sheriff tilted the brim of his hat and turned towards the flashing lights of his car. His towering figure cast a large shadow across Mr. C.'s worried face as he closed the front door.

"We need to get this place on lockdown." Mr. C. grabbed his cellphone and handed it to Jack. "Here. Call your mother, and tell her that you're home with me. I'll finish checking the rooms at the end of the hallway and grab you some fresh clothes. Keep your gun close by."

"Yessir," Jack replied. As he dialed his mother's cellphone number, his father proceeded down the hallway with his gun in hand. Mrs. C. would probably be furious with both of them for leaving the hospital, but the pain medicine seemed to take the edge off of everything, including Jack's fear of his mother. "Hell hath no fury," he mumbled to himself as the phone began to ring.

Suddenly, a song began to play inside the house. It echoed down the hall, past the rooms, and bled into the den area where Jack waited with his ear to the phone. Mr. C. stopped in his tracks, quickly pivoting his body and the barrel of his gun towards the source of the sound. It was hauntingly familiar, but it took a second or two for Jack and his father to recognize it. It was Mrs. C.'s favorite song, "Smile" by Nat King Cole. She used to sing it to Jack every night before bed.

"Mom?" Jack dropped the phone and called out to his mother as he struggled to wheel himself down the hallway.

"Stay back, Jack!" Mr. C. commanded. He took one step forward into the master bedroom.

"Mom! Mom, is that you?" Jack wheeled faster and faster as he approached his parents' room. "What's happening, Dad?"

"Jack! Stop! Don't come any closer! You don't need to see this, Son!" Mr. C. began to sob hysterically as he dropped to his knees in the doorway. "Please, don't come any closer, Jack."

Jack couldn't help but push past his father, but perhaps he should have heeded those dire warnings. His mother was home. She'd been there the entire time. Assuming she'd gone for a drive, he and his father had neglected to search the garage for her vehicle. What was she doing? Jack's eyes were wide with shock and horror. Who knows how long she'd been there. A couple hours? A few minutes? There were more books and pages spread about this room, across the floor, and under the bed. It looked like a tornado had ripped through, unleashing its wrath on specific, targeted objects. Old newspaper clippings and articles written about the hollow were among the cluttered chaos.

Jack's discombobulated eyes continued to glance from one antiquated artifact to the next. There were dated sketches and crudely drawn maps of the old church, the tree, the graveyard, and what appeared to be a tunnel system that ran the length of the hollow. Of course, Jack had never seen the grimoire, but he imagined some of the blood-spattered pages on the floor might belong to a wicked book like that. Finally, Jack's bemused eyes fell upon that which warped his mind and bewildered his psyche the most, his dead mother.

She hung upside down from the corner bed post, her stiff, blue neck craned against the cold, hard floor at an odd angle, glaring into nothingness with her lifeless eyes. Her bare breasts and face were awash with her own blood and oozing, black shit. Gravity took hold and pulled various excrements from the gaping cavity carved into her abdomen. It was a savagely, sanguinary disembowelment that rivaled that of the famous

Roman orator, Cato. She was tethered to the top of the wooden bedpost not by rope, but by her own stringy entrails, a dangling, corded, cocoon corpse crudely wrapped in several unraveling feet of her own feces-filled intestines.

Mr. C. sobbed the loudest when he identified the bloody Bowie blade his wife used to butcher herself as his own. She was strung up like a pale, plastic puppet and the demented Dream Demon, her puppeteer. Jack held the back of his hand to his retching, open mouth. Each involuntary gag reflex sent soured stomach acid into the back of his burning throat. Already, there was a putrescent smell about the room. It suddenly occurred to Jack that this was something pop-culture horror movies rarely seemed to accurately describe. The smell associated with a dead human was awful, a butchered body like this was unbearable, but a zombified, walking corpse could probably carry a stench potent enough to completely incapacitate a person.

"Jack. Son, we need to leave this room." Dry heaves and groanings were the only replies that Mr. C. received from his son. "Jack! Now! Please, goddammit!"

Mr. C. fought through his tears, trying to sound more assertive and fatherly. He knew it was too late. Seeing his mother like this would scar his son for life, but staying there wasn't doing him any good. Something happens to the look of a human being when they die. When the soul finally leaves the body, it looks like it was never alive. Maybe that's why wax museums are so creepy. No matter how good the wax figure, it never quite captures the essence of life.

Grief is a strange, unquantifiable sickness; Mr. C. felt his own will to live weaken with each fleeting moment. The sudden passing of a loved one can leave you feeling spellbound. Helplessly, you watch the bluing cold skin and the dreaded bloat of death that quickly swells from within, leaving the slightly phlegmatic face even less recognizable than before. It leaves your wheels spinning as your mind tries to come to terms with your own miserable mortality, survivor's guilt, and the ever-dimming light of the soul that once inhabited the now inanimate, morbid meat bag lying at your feet. To say it is the cruelest form of torture, to witness such a thing, would be the understatement of the century. You never really know the feeling, not until it's you standing there, staring into the nullity, the nothingness that inevitably engulfs all of our loved ones. And even then, you're never ready to smell the pungent rot that creeps through the void and into your sinus cavity.

"Focus up, Kid!" Mr. C. snapped out of his own trancelike state and had no intention of allowing his son's mind to wander any further into the darkness. "I need you to show me that photograph on your phone. With all of these articles and maps of the hollow here, it seems your mother was onto something. She was piecing things together." Mr. C. pulled Jack out of the bedroom and into the hallway, turning him towards his own room. "From what I've gathered about this demonic entity so far, it should only be able to attack people in their dreams. It seems it's becoming stronger with each...I mean, there wasn't enough time for your mother to fall asleep...She was so angry when she left the hospital." Mr. C. stopped himself from speaking. Jack couldn't bear to hear about his mother or anything of the sort. He was absolutely broken. They were both broken, but still he questioned beneath his breath, "To what end?"

"Here. I don't want to look at it." Jack handed his phone to his father.

Mr. C.'s eyes began to water as he looked down at the photo. It was, without a doubt, the girl he saw crawling through Jack's window. Her neck looked twisted and dislocated, just the same. Her eyes bulged from her skull, and bones protruded from her flesh. All of it was the same.

"I'm starting to think that Amelia isn't as innocent as we've been led to believe," Mr. C. mumbled. He noticed a bloody fingerprint on the back of the phone.

"Dad, I need to see Paige." Jack hung his head in sadness as he lethargically slipped into a t-shirt and slowly struggled to put on a pair of loose jogging pants.

"Son, I don't think it's a good time…" Mr. C. stared at the blood on the cellphone and wondered what his wife was doing with it. It seemed she knew more about the hollow than she'd ever revealed to anyone, including Mr. C. himself. Was the dybbuk causing her to tear through the house? Was it trying to destroy evidence of its existence?

"Dad! I need to see her!" Jack yelled, pleading from frustration and melancholic hysteria.

"Alright, Jack. I'll take you to see her." Mr. C. placed his son's phone into his pocket next to the folded grimoire page. He helped Jack get dressed and reluctantly followed him down the hallway. Deep down, he worried about Paige, too.

Chapter 19

Emotionless, Paige rose from her blood-stained bed leaving the soggy, cold sheets behind. She could feel various indentations on her neck as she lightly grazed her delicate fingertips across the dimpled bite marks. Her hair was an absolute mess, and she knew her mother would be displeased if she returned to the party in such an unpresentable manner. Paige proceeded to the bathroom, removing her torn, cum-crusted underwear and began fixing her bedraggled hair and costume.

"Anything to please you, Mother." She took a deep breath and slowly stumbled into the busy hallway.

The house was still inundated with creepy creatures and monstrous mischief-makers noisily conversing over drug-fueled rants and raves. It was alive with entrancing lights and throbbing with devilish tunes. Each color seemed to burn its way through the misty atmosphere and resonate more deeply within Paige's post-intoxicated mind. Each fluid wave of sound intimately reverberated through her bones like the song of an ethereal instrument. Her hips swayed uncontrollably and her wild eyes wandered aimlessly around the room. That is, until she set her gaze upon a grotesque gaggle of ghouls congregating around contraband on a crimson glass table. Their semi-translucent altar was covered in lines of ivory-white powder that glowed beneath the ultraviolet lights, accompanied by shiny, silver razor blades that glistened with each cut.

"I'm only paying for half since I wasn't her first." Paige heard a familiar voice in the distance as she buried her face in the snow. "She wasn't as special as you promised."

"You slimy, mucilaginous piece of human waste! I gave you my daughter, and this is how you repay me? You want to screw me, too?"

Paige's eyes rolled back as she lifted her head from the table and dusted her nose. "Mom?"

She jolted to her feet, wobbling on her high heels until she regained balance. Her skin burned; suddenly her body felt so warm, too warm. Paige had an overwhelming surge of liquid energy bursting throughout her body, but she had an even higher surge of paranoia breaching and bleeding into her brain. Why is everyone always watching me? She thought as the cluster of critters cluttered around the cocaine longingly reached out for her dress. No, I have to see my mother. I can't stay.

"Mom!" Paige called out as she quickly promenaded through the dancing demons and Moloch worshipers in the gossamer-thin clouds of fog.

"Paige! What are you doing?" Her mother nabbed a flash drive and a small stack of printed photographs from the masked man and quickly reached out to wipe the remaining visible powder from Paige's nose.

"Why'd you do it, Mom? I know it was you who gave me away. I know it was you that doomed my baby with your poison." Paige's bloodshot eyes cried beneath the blitzkrieg of pulsating lights. For a moment, she swore she saw her father in those photographs with underage boys but couldn't be sure. "I know I've always been a disappointment to you. I was never pretty enough, popular enough, thin enough..."

Paige's voice trailed as she raised a stolen razor blade to examine it. She watched the dizzying array of colors and lights reflect from its silver surface until the right angle revealed her own lackluster reflection. Then, with the devil in her eyes, she looked up at her mother and began violently hacking through her pinafore dress and slicing away the bulging, yellowy fat layers of her own stomach. Mistaking it for an elaborate Halloween hoax, a small group of the paganistic party-goers gathered around Paige, cheering and screaming as she scraped and peeled away the fatty flesh from her boney torso. In truth, no one knew if this morbid act of self-mutilation was real or just another adverse side-effect of a terrible concoction of psychedelic entheogens, stimulants, and nasty narcotics. Perhaps, it was not knowing that really tickled their fancies.

"Paige! Stop! Somebody, get help!" her mother screamed in absolute horror. Terrified and confused, the masked rapist slowly backed away from the center of the crowded circle.

"Am I skinny enough now, Mommy?" Paige clutched a slippery slab of her own fileted skin and meat; blood streamed down her legs and pooled in large puddles around her ruby red heels. With a slap and a hard thud, she feverishly dropped to her knees, slipping and sloshing around in her own slick blood. "I won't cover up the flaws between my thighs anymore, Mother." Kneeling, Paige opened up her tiny legs and butchered them to the bone. "I'm always so hungry, but you never let me eat." Gashing, carving, and vigorously mangling her fragile flesh, Paige held hashed chunks of her legs in the palms of her blood-filled hands. "I don't want to be hungry anymore." Paige looked up, smiled at her horrified, speechless mother, and ferociously consumed the greasy clumps of cleaved leg meat, clinching the squishy bits between her pearly white teeth.

"Paige?" Jack called from his chair as his father wheeled him through snaking lines of pie-eyed wino, politicians and befuddled, billionaire drug addicts.

Archfiend lovers laid with adolescent boys and scantily clad girls in various ill-lit corners of the hellish house. Jack's medicine was wearing away, and the pain was quickly returning. The disorientating bombardment of loud sounds and flickering lights caused the sour in his stomach to, once again, tickle the back of his throat. The images of his mother's lifeless corpse still festered in the back of his mind--and that smell. He didn't know why, but he swore he could smell it again.

"Dad, I think I'm going to be sick." Once more, Jack held the back of his hand to his mouth, fighting the urge to dry heave.

"I know, Son. We'll find her and get out of here ASAP, but I don't think I could live with myself if I left without calling Stone. Some of these kids are younger than you." Mr. C. removed his cellphone from his pocket. Suddenly, it began to ring. *Now's not a good time, Max,* he thought as he sent the call to his non-existent voicemail.

He quickly dialed the sheriff's personal cell number and held the phone tightly to his ear. "Stone, it's Philip Carter. I'm going to need you to get down here…Yeah, that's right. Bring back up and lots of cuffs… Yeah, you're going to need them…You'll see when you get here. I'll text the address to you."

Jack continued forward as his father fell further and further behind. The fresh smell of death was getting stronger, and he struggled to keep the acidic worms of vomit from spewing out his mouth. A thick gathering of freakishly costumed men and women stood before him. A strange mixture of screams and cheers filled the air, and it rode alongside that awful, lingering smell. A peculiar man with half a mask walked backwards and bumped into Jack's injured leg.

"Ow! Watch where you're going, you piece of shit!" Jack yelled out in pain, but the man paid him no mind. He seemed too terror-stricken to retort, and that worried Jack even more. "Paige!" Jack called once more, yelling at the top of his longs.

Snapping out of a trance, the masked man turned to him, looking down with half a grin. "You must be Jack. If it makes you feel any better, the crazy bitch moaned your name every time she orgasmed. She's quite the squirter, even when she's drugged out of her mind."

"What the fuck did you just say to me?" Jack's eyes had never opened so wide in his life.

"Jack!" There was a pleading call from within the circle of people. It sounded like Paige.

"Paige! I'm here!" He called back and forcefully wheeled himself forward, bumping his bandaged leg into bystanders without a wince. "I'm here, Babe!"

He made one last push through the crowded circle, and there she was. Every fight, every lie, every kiss, and every time they made love flashed before his eyes like a grainy, black and white movie. Jack's fragile, foggy mind simply could not process what his eyes were seeing. Paige looked up at him from the floor. Her mutilated flesh dangled from her tiny bones. She was holding a razor blade to the hard part of her throat, just below the Adam's apple.

"Jack, you were going to be a father…"

"Paige? God, what happened to you? What are you saying to me? Please, put down the blade." Jack fell to the floor in tears, landing on his wound. He crawled closer to Paige, swimming through puddles of her blood.

"Jack, they killed our baby. My mother…That man...They poisoned our child!" Paige screamed bloody murder as she drove the small razor through her throat. She sawed away at her esophagus, pulling it completely across her neck until she drowned in what little blood she had left.

"No! God, no!" Jack reached for her guillotine-like arm, struggling to stop the self-inflicted torture, but it was far too late. Even if he'd managed to halt the barbaric hacking, it was clear that she would have succumbed to dozens of other fatal lacerations.

Jack yelled out in emotional and physical agony. He caught her limp torso in his arms just before it hit the slippery ground. It was the same as his mother. Something happened to her lifeless body as her soul left the earth. It seemed so inanimate. A light turned on in the distance, and another putrescent wave of death overwhelmed Jack's senses. Her corpse looked fake, but it certainly smelled real. He heaved, vomiting green and yellow stomach fluid all over the blood-covered floor. Mr. C. and Paige's father simultaneously happened upon the gut-churning scene with Sheriff Stone; the sickened crowd dispersed into a frenzy of freaks. Cuffs in hand, Stone's deputies swarmed the house.

"Arrest that man! He drugged and assaulted my daughter!" Paige's mother screamed and pointed at the man with half a mask, double-crossing her accomplice. He tried to run, but was met with extreme prejudice as Sheriff Stone grabbed him around his neck and threw him to the cold floor.

"You're not going anywhere, you sick son of a bitch!" Stone rolled the man onto his stomach and bent his arms behind his back. "None of you are going anywhere! Stay put!"

The man's mask was violently ripped from his face during the altercation, revealing his identity to the crowd. He was nothing more than a nameless intern working under Paige's father. It seems he wasn't the only one working under her father. The photos showed that much to be true.

Mr. C.'s pockets continued to buzz with calls from Max. This time it was Jack's phone that rang. "Max…Calm down, Son…Are you hurt... Thomas?...Oh no, Max…"

"What's all that about, Philip?" Stone looked over at Mr. C. with a look of dread upon his face.

"Jack's friends across town." Mr. C.'s tired eyes seemed to disappear in the dark circles that hung beneath them. "There's nothing we could do. It seems everyone who's come into contact with this thing is dying."

"Mr. Carter, what is it that you're not telling me? You know something about this shit. Don't you?" Stone looked Mr. C. dead in the eyes, but he did not respond.

"My wife's dead. That's what I know." As Mr. C. spoke, the life was instantly drained from his face, appearing even more lugubrious than before.

Stone's jaw visibly dropped so far it nearly unhinged itself from his thin face.

Mr. C. averted his teary eyes and left the room. He massaged the tension from his wrinkling forehead as he leaned against a large, sturdy table. At the head of it was an open book filled with stained pages of odd scribblings, strange incantations, and eccentric rituals. One such ritual depicted a seance involving a eucharist-shaped offering to a demonic entity.

The recipe for the spell was listed in various languages and involved several godawful body fluids. Mr. C. was aware of a tunnel beneath the hollow, but this seemed to depict an additional secret chamber beneath the bleeding tree just like the one described by Thomas. These pages appeared to compliment the ones in his private library, but even more concerning was their uncanny resemblance to the grimoire page he'd taken from Emerlyn. They may be the missing pieces his wife hoped to find before she died.

"Don't let this bitch go free!" Jack screamed through his tears as he pointed at Paige's mother. "Paige told me you arranged this! She told me she was supposed to have my child, but you poisoned our baby! I hope you get what's coming for you!" Jack pulled at his wheelchair, dragging it through Paige's crimson blood and his green puke. He struggled to crawl back into the seat but refused help from nearby deputies. "I hope you rot in Hell. You fucking worthless trash."

Chapter 20

Max stepped into the living room. His mother was passed out on the couch, two bottles of wine--one empty and one nearly so--on the coffee table. He wasn't used to her being home at night, or at all; but she'd raced back after Thomas's death. Death. It's such a short word for something so permanent. What little life there was left in their hollow home had all but died with Thomas. Max finished what was left in his mother's glass and picked up both bottles, turning off the incandescent lamp next to her limp body and covering her with a fuzzy blanket before continuing into the kitchen.

The room was dark, so he switched on the overhead oven light, flooding the room with an amber glow. Max tossed the empty bottle into the trash and took another drink before setting the second bottle on the table. He opened the oven and stared…leftover tendies and tots. He didn't really want any of it, but Thomas would probably tell him to eat something.

Emotionally and physically exhausted, he sank into a cold chair and waited for his food to finish reheating. He didn't want to think, to remember. He didn't want to rest--or worse, sleep--because every time he closed his eyes he saw Thomas. Not having him around was far scarier than any Dream Demon.

Max shut his eyelids tightly, hoping to squeeze the thoughts of his brother's crushed corpse, crimson-colored blood, and fractured teeth out of his own mind. He drank more of the wine; that would at least dull his senses so everything wouldn't feel so sharp, even just for a while. Still, there was a twitching in his left eye that mimicked the rhythm of his dead brother's convulsions. Max wasn't sure how long he'd been sitting there when he heard his mother stir in the next room, the outline of her figure wandering around in the darkness.

"I made some food, Ma," Max called out.

The reply was muffled, incoherent, and he heard labored footsteps shuffle toward the kitchen. A loud buzzing made Max jump. The timer. He hurried to turn it off. He took the food from the oven and looked into the living room to find his mother right where he'd left her. It was all messing with his head. That story, the tree, Jack, Thomas.

Thomas.

A tear slid down his cheek, and Max quickly wiped it away, cursing. He was the man of the house now, and he had to take care of things. He squeezed ketchup onto the plate next to the food and sat down to eat. Max dipped a chicken tender into the ketchup and took a bite. He paused, staring at the food in his hand. A red droplet fell to the plate, and he thought of Thomas all over again.

Blood everywhere. The image of his brother, or what had been left of him, flooded his mind. Perhaps, some mustard to compliment the yellowish fluids that seeped from his brother's body? He hadn't been a body anymore. Thomas had been in pieces. Bile rose in Max's throat, and he rushed to the garbage can. He spit out the chicken and vomited what little remained in his stomach from earlier that day. He leaned against the cool, kitchen cabinet.

He tried to call Emerlyn again, but no one answered. Max slid his phone into his pocket and pushed himself off the floor. He dumped the rest of the food into the trash and made his way down the hall.

Thomas's door was slightly ajar; and Max quietly slipped inside, shutting the door behind him. A poster of a malevolent-looking duck hung on the wall; and, despite his grief, the caption written across it, 'They Are Watching', brought a sad smile to his face. He looked through the various books Thomas had, flipping through page after page of weird-looking creatures. The only one he recognized was Bigfoot. None of it made any sense to him, but it was a connection to his brother. Once more, Max squeezed his eyes shut and slammed the book closed.

"What the hell were you doing out there, Thomas?" he asked, his voice sounding unnaturally loud in the silence.

He sat on Thomas's bed, grabbed a pillow, and propped himself against the wall. Max felt the same weight and weariness from before. He remembered what Mr. C. said about not falling asleep, but maybe if he just closed his eyes for a minute or two it would be okay.

A startling noise coming down the hall caught Max's attention. He listened closely. It was the sound of unsteady footsteps, much like those he thought he'd heard in the living room, and the steady thump of a hand against the wall.

"Ma?"

No answer. The noise continued to grow louder and closer before stopping outside the door. Max slowly stood and took a step toward it. He jumped and spun around when he heard the beeping sounds of Thomas's computer coming to life. With only one other lamp on, the screen cast an eerie glow across the empty room. He figured he must have knocked it out of sleep mode when he tossed the book back onto the desk. Images like those in the books flashed onto the screen. While he stared at them, they began to change. Instead of the pictures he'd seen in the book, they were all of Thomas and him. Max's chest tightened; it was becoming hard to breathe. They appeared, one after another, scrolling faster and faster until the screen went black. Max waited. It lit up again; and this time, instead of seeing Thomas's smiling face, he saw images of the accident. Thomas's body, battered, broken, and the way his eye dangled just outside the socket. It was crimson and shiny like some sort of morbid mirror ball suspended from the limb of a dying Krampus tree.

"What the fuck?" Max's head jerked around when he heard the creaking of the doorknob. He watched it turn slowly then come to a sudden stop.

Max felt his chest tighten and reached for his inhaler, taking two puffs. He stood, his eyes glued to the doorknob, waiting for whoever was on the other side of the door to open it. It had to be his mother; no one else was in the house. Why, then, did he feel so anxious inside? He was glad no one else was there to poke fun at his nervousness. He'd have denied it anyway, of course, especially if Paige or Emerlyn were around.

He took a few tentative steps toward the door and reached for the doorknob. Turning it quickly, he yanked the door open and looked into the hallway. Seeing no one, he ventured out, cautiously looking around and behind him. It reminded him of when he and Thomas were kids and would try to scare each other; and as ridiculous as he knew it was, for a second, it felt like his brother might jump out from behind the couch or something, just like old times.

Once Max reached the living room, he saw his mother was still passed out on the couch, which only confused him more. More rustling in the kitchen caught his attention, so he followed the noise. As he got closer to it, Max realized it sounded like someone was unlocking the back door.

"Shit," he whispered.

He took one tentative step after another, not really wanting to know who was in the house but also acknowledging that there was no one else around to handle it. The only means of self-defense available to him were those awful, cheap ninja swords in his room and that tiny stun gun. Neither of which were reliable enough to do any good. The back door stood open; Max was certain someone had been in the house. He pulled his phone from his pocket; he should call 911, right?

"Oh no. I'm becoming a statistic. I'm relying on the government to save me," Max whispered under his breath.

Max stuck his head outside and looked around. It was dark, but the full moon lit up parts of the yard and field behind it. The lunar light was bright enough for him to see clearly; but it also created pockets of darkness, providing the perfect cover for an unwanted trespasser. Ignoring the cruel irony, he zipped up his *Left 4 Dead* hoodie and took a few more steps forward, scanning around and in front of him while staying close enough to the house to make a run for it. Max dialed.

"911, what's your emergency?" the operator asked.

"I think someone was in my house," he answered, his voice low.

"Okay, what's your name?" she asked.

"Max."

"Okay, Max, I'm Lilly. Can you tell if the person is still there?" the 911 operator asked.

"It doesn't look like it," Max began, taking his first step outside. "I don't see anyone." He started to wonder if he'd imagined the whole thing.

"We're sending an officer to check; stay inside and close the door. I'll remain on the line with you," she explained.

Too late, Max thought. "Uh-huh."

Right now he needed to find something to use to defend himself in case somebody really was outside the house.

"Everything okay, Max?" He almost forgot that he was on the phone with 911.

"Yeah," he said quietly.

"A unit is on its way," she said.

Max made his way to the shed in the back corner of the yard and went inside. He set his phone on the small gardening table and looked for a pair of shears, a trowel, anything. A rusty rake fell to the filthy floor, stirring dust and startling him. Max bumped into the cluttered table, knocking his phone to the gravelly ground, and before he knew it, he'd already stepped on it. He heard the loud crunch of his shattering screen and winced.

"Shit," he said, picking it up. The phone was destroyed; so much for 911. He patted his pockets and realized he'd dropped his inhaler, too.

Max felt around for it and found it wedged between a tin bucket and the shelves where his mother kept extra planters. He wiped it off and shoved it into his pocket again, but not before taking two more puffs. His lungs felt tight, so he made sure to breathe in deeply. It burned; but sometimes that happened so Max ignored it. He grabbed the flashlight and decided to check the property once more before making his way back toward the house. At this point, he guessed no one was around; but he wanted to be sure. Max gripped the shears in one hand and stepped out of the shed.

The property was fairly large and backed up against a field. Max shone the light across it and squinted. The burning in his throat spread to his lungs, making him cough. Max coughed up phlegm, trying to muffle the sound with his elbow, just in case someone really was out there. He spit onto the ground and continued walking the back length of the yard. Relieved at seeing nothing in the field, he turned his attention to the side of the property near the driveway. In truth, he didn't really want to find anyone there, but he remembered Thomas's advice in the tunnel about controlling his overactive imagination and not being a coward.

Max coughed again, taking out his inhaler. The fear and stress were wreaking havoc on his asthma. He shook it, pressed the top, and breathed in. More burning.

Screw it, he thought. After a quick pass by the driveway, he headed back toward the house.

A coughing fit seized his body; and he doubled over, placing his hands on his knees to steady himself. He spit again, more this time, and blinked to clear his vision. Max straightened his posture and tried to focus on the back door to his house. In his peripheral, he saw a shadowy figure move quickly in his direction. Max picked up the pace, stumbling toward his house, coughing harder.

He tripped, dropping the flashlight as he struggled to regain his footing. He could feel the figure getting closer and knew he'd be safe if he could just get back inside the damn house. The police were on their way, right? Another coughing fit wracked his body; and he stumbled again, clawing his way to the back stoop. He turned to see the figure approaching more slowly now, casually taking its time.

Max rolled onto his back, gasping for fresh air. With each hacking cough, he spit more blood, staining the front of his hoodie. A can of commercial grade insecticide fell from his hand where the inhaler was supposed to be. His chest heaved as he struggled to get precious oxygen into his lungs, blood splattered on his face and clothes. As Max's vision blurred and the light faded; the figure came to a stop, standing over him. He was unable to make out a face; it seemed more specter than solid. The only thing he could see, before his world went black, was that it was smiling a toothy grin.

Chapter 21

Emerlyn gasped for air as she awoke, startled from a dead sleep. Saved from suffocation by another night terror, she thought as she massaged the pulsating headache from the bridge of her nose. The muted television flashed in black and white as the horror movie marathon silently crept along with *The Wolf Man*. The living room was empty and the air was cold and still. Almost, too still. Where'd they go? Emerlyn squinted her sleepy eyes as she glanced over at the spot where her parents once laid. Forsaken again, I suppose.

It was nothing new, to be left to fend for herself, especially in times of need. Her mother and father deflected most of their responsibilities by telling Emerlyn to pray about it. It was getting late, but she felt groggier than usual. It was hard to tell if she'd even woken up. Maybe, it was all still part of a dream, a never-ending nightmare.

"What the hell is going on?" she muttered as she stood next to the empty couch.

The room began to sway from side to side, and the ground seemed to swell beneath her feet. She reached for the safety of her cross, but her breast was bare. Emerlyn struggled to keep her balance atop the shifting sands. Then, the burning realization of what she'd done quickly set her soul ablaze. Like the start of an untamed wildfire, anxiety smoldered then swirled into a whirlwind of panic, spreading across the surface of her skin but burning from within.

"My cross!"

Emerlyn started towards the hallway, struggling to walk a straight line. She knew it was unsafe to remove the crucifix, unwise to reject its protection. The necklace had acted as an amulet against the unknown that roamed the earth and tiptoed through her room at night. She believed it was the very thing that kept her safe from demonic visitors, too. As she stumbled into the pitch-black hallway, she clumsily ran her fingers along the cold, textured wall searching for a light switch. Normally, she could quickly make it to the bathroom by muscle memory, alone. Tonight, her mind was foggy, and her body was completely uncooperative. After what seemed like a lifetime of searching, she finally felt the frigid metal of a doorknob in the palm of her quivering hand. She turned it and quickly entered the room. Her fingers fiddled around in the dark until they fell upon the familiar feeling of braided rope. It was stuck on something. Emerlyn pulled at it with all her might, and with a loud snap it finally broke free. The ground was still wobbly as she donned the rope around her neck.

Creak. Crack. Creak. Crack. That haunting sound was back, and this time it seemed like it was closer than ever. It was so close that she could feel it. The sound emanated below her wriggling toes. Creak. Crack. Creak. Crack.

Suddenly, the floor fell from beneath her, and the necklace felt more like a noose! As the rope burned and cut its way through her tiny neck, it quickly cinched and squeezed the fragile life from her ailing body. In a sick twist of fate, Emerlyn found herself hanging from a support beam, a pull cord crudely wrapped around her neck. She was dangling mere inches from her grandmother's rocking chair, and there was absolutely nothing she could do about it. The process was slow and the pain, excruciating. The full weight of Emerlyn's body crushed her larynx, collapsed her veins, and ripped the arteries in her neck, causing an immense pressure to develop behind her bulging, bleeding eyes and inside her swelling brain. Before the last bit of oxygen was constricted from her airways, she swore she saw Amelia standing there, smiling. Or was it something else? Then, she went limp and everything went black. Golden urine and chocolate colored feces dribbled down her legs and onto the cockeyed chair below.

A strangely familiar face, licked by a thousand blue flames, flickered in the darkness, appearing just beyond Emerlyn's crooked, cold gaze. Never stagnant, it flashed back and forth between an immaculate, masculine creature and a grotesque abomination with malefic eyes--a fallen angel. The entity's body seemed to rapidly materialize out of the darkest of shadows, a Vantablack mass. One moment, it appeared like a well-groomed adult male. The next was more angelic, yet hellish in nature, scarred from countless wars fought in innumerable dimensions. However it chose to take shape, it always exuded a sense of strength and an overwhelming presence.

"My Dear, you're lying in limbo between life and Death. At least, the treasonous sedative you've ingested to betray your conscious thoughts is no longer relevant, not here. I know you can see otherworldly things, Emerlyn. So I've no doubt you can see ME, now. Please, pay no attention to the way I might appear to you. The human mind is incapable of fully perceiving a being such as myself. Come to think of it, there are no other beings quite like ME. Oh, and do ME a favor. Please, don't call ME Satan. Contrary to popular belief, we are not the same entity. I'm not nearly as petty or repulsive!

No, I didn't venture all of this way to save you, Emerlyn. I'd never subscribe to a grandiose facade such as grace. Foolish! I'm simply using your mortal body as an insurance policy, a soiled, fleshy vessel of opportunity; and I will be your celestial liaison. It's quite obvious to ME that your soul is damned regardless. Seems it really does run in your blood. Your grandmother begged ME to tell you that she sends her love from Hell. But you and I know better. Don't we? If she really loved you, she wouldn't have taken her own life. I'm often blamed for mankind's sicknesses. I'm not the one who made you so feeble. The real cancer was inside her soul. It was always there, waiting. And I suppose most mortals were never meant to bear the burden of seeing the unseen. She lasted longer than you. Luckily, I have other plans for you, Emerlyn!

Don't look at ME with those lifeless, vitriolic eyes. I assure you, there is nothing sadistic about what I do. I'm just ME, a simple cog in the machine, a part of the equilibrium of space and time, here to tip the scales when necessary. Just as your ancestors in the hollow, you and your friends have upset the balance, awakening something you could not control or ever hope to understand. So here I am, tipping the scales, again, through you.

What? You didn't think I was going to get my little hands dirty, did you? No, my child. You did this, and you shall fix it. Consider it a professional courtesy. I delay your inevitable, miserable death for a

short while, and you stop this annoying little creature from wreaking havoc on mankind. It does ME no favors to have mortals cursing my name, blaming all of this on little old ME. It's not a good look for these hellions to be so overt. It creates too many diehard believers. Much better to be subtle about it. In spite of what you've been told, finesse and integrity are cherished in all realms. There are always rules. There must be symmetry.

By the way, the one you call Christ, he can hear you. We can all hear you. I guess he just doesn't feel much like talking to you. I don't blame him. Look at you, so pathetic! It is a wonderful irony that you were created in his image. In fairness, I'm not without my own inherent flaws, a victim of circumstance, I suppose. But at least I am not bound or chained to one realm. How can I put this? Think of ME as a well traveled socialite, a diplomat between higher frequency beings and their lower frequency counterparts. And of course, everything in between. Just as there are different shades of shadows in the night, there are different degrees of darkness throughout all planes of existence. Some cast a silhouette far darker than others.

Now, that we've been formally introduced...Let's get down to brass tacks. You will follow the Dream Demon, the one who mimics the appearance of that poor little pagan, Amelia. Such a shame she had to take the fall for her curiosity of the Devil. You'll need to find the dybbuk's next host and perform the live burial ritual. Of course, it will be amusing to watch you complete the task with such an awful crick in your neck. I suppose you'll have to be creative!

Wondering how I know about the ever-elusive grimoire? Who do you think crafted such a fine handbook? And in years past, who might have whispered into the ears of ancient man to use such a fantastical tome? Yes, yours truly. There were other beatific documents spread throughout the sands of time, each serving a different purpose. I was careful never to put more than one book on the same landmass. Still, I never imagined your kind would so foolishly misuse such an empyreal gift. I was simply sharing seraphic wisdom that I'd gathered in my travels, creating a conduit of communication, and, of course, having a little fun.

After Amelia was ironically hanged for ignorantly invoking

Hell on Earth, performing a forbidden ritual beneath the bleeding tree, Holcomb continued to see her specter haunting his dreams, draining his will to live. Only, it wasn't her at all. Holcomb lacked the wisdom to properly execute the demon inside the witch. Only a shell of Amelia's former self remained. It was the tiniest of whispers that finally motivated her partner in crime, the warlock Philip Carter, to take care of that nasty loose end, Holcomb. It was the price he paid for losing the battle against the Dream Demon, and the pastor died by the hands of his best friend.

Unfortunately, there are still those among you that have striven to destroy the book's few surviving pages. Jack's mother, Alice, for instance. A secret, collateral descendant of Amelia. She's been a real pain in my neck! I'm sure you can appreciate the sentiment. Out of fear and slightly vengeful motives, she foolishly misused precious information gathered from her husband's little library, a rather excitingly eclectic collection. Alice aimed to shred accurate recreations of invaluable maps and descriptions of grimoire pages. Suspicious of surviving documents, she even went so far as to destroy the crumbling undercroft and evidence of Philip Carter's very existence. Her blind stupidity may have worked in our favor, as she was too busy desecrating meaningless graves to ever find the real ritual page hidden in Amelia's cabin. It is the most important document in the fight against this particular demonic entity. I took great care to lead you to it, and still you failed to use it! That petty impersonator, a sorry excuse for a demon, even tempted you to destroy the page during your little visit to the secret chamber. There are few methods quite so effective, Emerlyn! Vivisepulture, as your special friend would call it, is quite permanent, lest you break the seal of the tomb when the veil is thin. It seems fate led you to the hollow on the most unfortunate of nights. Perhaps, it was your destiny to hang here before me.

On this faux-hallowed night, I think you'll find fate and freewill leaving you in quite the crippling conundrum. You'll have to make a choice. Complete the ritual as written, burying the live host until the next unfortunate soul scampers into the demonic hornets nest on some unforeseen Halloween. If you do this, you'll be tasked with preserving the surviving ritual page. Or, my dear Emerlyn, you can

end it once and for all! To do this, you'll have to trap the parasite and the person in the secret chamber beneath the bleeding tree. It is the throbbing heart, the lifeline, and the womb of the summoned entity. Only, there can the demon be sent back to Hell, where I will travel to rip it limb from limb in the most pleasurably, painful of fashions. If successful, you will be tasked with destroying all remaining pages of the grimoire, including the burial ritual and those held by some of the more elite members of your community. We shall leave no trace of this disasterpiece behind. But of course, there's a catch! The more permanent solution is only viable until 3:33 am. That is when the Devil's clock resets, and the drawbridge between realms is lifted. Quite unfortunate timing, I know.

I heard some even more unfortunate news about your special friend, Thomas. It's such a shame, really. I had high hopes of continuing to torment the two of you with bits of forbidden knowledge. And I thought the bats were a nice touch. Wouldn't you agree? Admittedly, bats are more suited for a belfry. I did what I could to help you discover the page in the cabin, and now his death is your greatest failure. Whatever you decide to do, this time, do take care to finish the job before dying on ME.

There are six ritualistic suicides from the grimoire: Death by crushing, decapitation, disembowelment, poison, mutilation, and strangulation. I'm sure you can guess which one pertains to you, Emerlyn. With each successful self-sacrifice, the dybbuk grows stronger, shifting its shape to suit its cause, and influencing its next host more easily, especially on a night such as Halloween. There is little resistance left to slow the parasite's pace. Had I not paid you a little visit, you would have been the sixth and final death, rendering all victim souls damned forever and granting the demon the freedom to walk on your plane of existence without oversight, a real logistical nightmare for the both of us. If you choose the more permanent approach to your task, I'll see to it that all souls involved are returned to their proper places. If the dybbuk successfully takes a sixth host by method of strangulation, there is nothing more I can do for you. Just think of Thomas's poor soul as it rots in the belly of the beast.

Finish the job, Emerlyn. Then, do what thou wilt. I care not. Now, wake up! Time is running out..."

"Lucifer," Emerlyn hoarsely whispered as her limp body crashed to the unforgiving floor, defibrillating her dying heart and reanimating her lifeless corpse beside the excrement-covered rocking chair.

She gagged and coughed as she pulled the coarse binding from her bruised throat and crawled into the hallway. With a pounding headache, she continued to drag her crippled body behind her until she reached the trash can under the bathroom sink. Emerlyn quickly grabbed the crucifix from the garbage and held it to her aching chest as she continued to gasp for precious air. She sat against the wall and kicked the bathroom door shut while she cried, cradling the cold cross.

"Thomas, I need you." Emerlyn burst into tears, hoping her muttered words would somehow transcend death and find a way to Thomas. "Please, come back to me. I can't do this alone." She sobbed as the dread of loneliness set inside her bones. Lucifer had granted her a choice, but it was no choice at all. Midnight was quickly approaching, and Emerlyn knew what she had to do. "3:33am...It seems I'm bound to the devil's clock for the next few hours."

Chapter 22

Emerlyn's cold fingers trembled across her phone as she repeatedly called Max and Paige, reaching nothing but the unmoved sounds of an apathetic voicemail. She feared the worst for them, but her efforts were in vain. Nervousness bled from her broken body like an open wound, and the crippling tremors intensified. It's almost midnight. Those words played on a never-ending loop inside Emerlyn's aching head.

With nowhere to go and no one else to turn to, she reached out to Mr. C. He was the only adult in the world that would believe she'd actually been visited by Lucifer. Even stranger was the feeling of being temporarily pardoned from Death, saved from eternal darkness by the light of the morning star. The only other person on the planet who would listen to such a ludicrous recount was Thomas, but he'd been taken from her. Even his essence was stripped away from Emerlyn's plane of existence. She'd often dreaded the thought of losing his companionship but hoped her curse of seeing the unseen would, at least, allow a partial continuation of their partnership. Even that was impossible as long as the dybbuk laid claim to his soul.

After several failed attempts, Mr. C. finally answered his phone; but his voice sounded nearly as hollow and distant as the others' voicemails. The background noise was disproportionately chaotic, and that stark contrast left Emerlyn feeling even more unsettled than before. He didn't go into detail but explained that Thomas, Paige, his wife, and a local deputy had all passed away within hours. Emerlyn reluctantly imagined the horrible ways they must have met their end as Lucifer's recitation of the grimoire replayed inside her head: Death by crushing, decapitation, disembowelment, poison, mutilation, and strangulation. Her mind went to even darker places as she weighed the possibility of Max's fate. She knew time was running out; but if she was going to seek help from Mr. C., she'd have to meet him at the morgue.

Jack sat by Paige's sheet-covered corpse in the funeral home. Her body was not yet properly prepared for viewing, but the mortician was kind enough to allow him a little more time to make peace with her. He left her frigid blue hand exposed for Jack to hold. Besides, Halloween had provided more than enough work to keep the undertaker busy.

Mr. C. stood, shaking just outside the crematorium where his wife's remains were turned into ash. Thomas would most likely follow suit as his face was horribly disfigured and unfit for viewing. Unfortunately, Deputy Huey's body was deemed mostly unsalvageable. Only a few bits and pieces would be burned to display at his memorial.

Emerlyn rubbed the dark, purple bruise around her aching neck as she pulled up to the deadhouse in her father's car. The old Havely Morgue was uncomfortably close to the outskirts of town and the threshold of the haunted hollow. Seemed that over the years, the only legitimate business that could survive in such close proximity to death was this creepy funeral parlor. Emerlyn hadn't realized it before, but most occupations around here were generational curses. For the Havely family, they were cursed to craft the coffin, perform burial rites, and execute the near equivalent of human taxidermy. The hammer on Ellis Havely's headstone was starting to make more sense. For all the morbid work they'd done, the Havely's would still be the ones to drive the final nails in her friends' coffins.

Only two dim lanterns illuminated the parking lot as the bashful Blue Moon tucked itself behind a blanket of cool clouds. It was an eerie sight to see so many vehicles parked outside a funeral home in the dead of night. Even more horrifying were the shadow figures that danced aimlessly in the darkness and trudged beneath the amber-colored lamps. Emerlyn closed her blue eyes, squeezing them tightly in hopes the spooks would make themselves scarce.

She killed the engine and raced towards the entrance of the mortuary. The faster she walked, the more it felt like something sinister was breathing down her neck, something wicked was whispering just behind her ears, and perhaps something preternatural pulling at her hair. She reached out and grabbed the door, yanking it by the metal handle with all her might; but it was locked. Her heart sank into the soles of her shoes as she desperately banged her fists on the freezing glass, begging for someone to let her inside. As she pulled at the doors, she could hear her coat pocket rattle from a bottle of pills she'd pretended to misplace days ago. Emerlyn half-expected the dreaded creaks and cracks of her grandmother's old rocking chair to accompany those ruffling rattles; and with that thought nesting itself deep inside the forefront of her befuddled brain, a large, gloved hand materialized out of the darkness, resting itself on her shoulder. The sheer weight of it pulled at the unlucky locks of hair that found themselves trapped beneath its hefty grip.

"You must be Emerlyn." A thunderous voice erupted from behind her, presumably the owner of the heavy hand that effortlessly pulled at her body.

Reluctantly, Emerlyn surrendered herself to the grasp and turned to see a monstrously large silhouette wearing a wide brimmed hat and an overcoat. It towered her by several feet and appeared heavier by far.

"I didn't mean to startle you, child. Mr. Carter said he was expecting you. Come around back; I'll show you to him."

"If you don't mind me asking, who are you, Sir?" Emerlyn's voice shuddered partly from the cold but mostly from the copious amounts of trepidation surging through her soul.

"Forgive an old man's manners. It's late and I am terribly tired. Feels like this night will never end! The name's Walter Havely, and I'm in the unfortunate business of undertaking the dead. Now, come with me. Let's get out of this cold before I find myself inside a casket of my own!"

Emerlyn's feet felt like lead, and she hesitated her first few steps towards the rear entrance of the large building. Rows of shining, silvery squares shimmered beneath a ghostly atmosphere as Walter and Emerlyn entered the morgue. The room held a soul-stirring chill that seemed to cut straight to the bone.

"Hurry now, Emerlyn! It does us no favors to linger in here. We might as well have waltzed our way into an industrial sized freezer or simply stayed outside."

The undertaker chuckled beneath his fogging breath as he led Emerlyn from the cold and into an adjacent room that wreaked of formaldehyde. There, Jack sat holding the hand of a corpse that was obscured from view.

"Jack?" Emerlyn's eyes instantly teared as she called out to him; but Jack was unresponsive, frozen in place like the other stiffs stricken by rigor mortis.

By the hypnotic look of terror and grief permanently painted across his face, she knew exactly who was under the white sheet. Not even the loss of his own mother could carve such a look into his sunken skin. Jack looked to have aged by at least ten years since the last time Emerlyn laid eyes upon him. She genuinely feared that the Dream Demon would come back to finish draining the life from his sad eyes.

"Best to leave him be for now. Hurry along, Emerlyn," The undertaker persisted. "Mr. Carter, your visitor is here." Havely's deep voice seemed to rattle the metallic instruments and fluid-filled jars that laid about the room as he and Emerlyn rounded the hallway near the crematorium; but Mr. C. remained silent. "Well, now. I'll leave you to it."

"Thank you, Mr. Walter." Emerlyn nodded as the undertaker vanished into the darkness of the doorway to the crematorium.

"Walter?" Mr. C. curiously inquired. "Who were you talking to, Emerlyn?"

Emerlyn craned her neck in confusion; but before she could muster up the nerve to mutter a single syllable, she knew something was terribly wrong. It seemed she'd been talking to another apparition. It was getting harder to tell the living from the dead. Still, there was something else in the hallway, something far worse than the benign being that escorted her to Mr. C. The air was stale; and a sudden, overwhelming bombardment of sound filled the air around Jack's father. It was nearly indescribable and only comparable to the intense fluttering noise experienced when sticking your head out the window of a fast moving vehicle. It was a rapidly pulsating swishing and swirling of high and low frequency clangor that wrapped itself around Mr. C.

"What is it Emerlyn?" He furrowed his brow. "What's going on?"

"What do you mean, Mr. C.?" Emerlyn feared that her looks or thoughts had betrayed her.

She strained the muscles in her face to refrain from wincing at the perverse noises that molested her once virgin ears. Far worse than the violating sounds she heard was the decrepit little thing that she saw. Whether it was Emerlyn's flirtation with suicide, Lucifer's otherworldly touch, or some combination thereof, whatever the reason, the suicide dybbuk no longer masked its appearance to her. Gone was the shadow and torn skin of Amelia that once covered its grotesque anatomy.

"I mean, why did you drive all this way in the dead of night? I thought we agreed you'd lock yourself somewhere safe," Mr. C. replied. "You must have something you need to tell me. Right? You're acting very strangely, but who could blame you?" He paused, thinking of his wife and Jack. The silence that filled his heart and mind was laced with an unbearable weight of guilt and sadness. "Look, I'm sorry I've failed you. I'm sorry I failed everyone."

Though she felt Mr. C.'s immense sorrow, Emerlyn struggled to turn her gaze away from the disfigured demon. Contrary to the ancient artistic renditions of demonic entities she'd seen in books and paintings, the dybbuk had no humanoid features. It did not have eyes, neither did it have two legs or two hands. The being was ugly to Emerlyn's mortal senses. It was absolutely repulsive, but not in the way she'd imagined it would be.

There were no words in the English language that could accurately describe or quantify the thing that had attached itself to Mr. C. At first, it clung to his inner thighs, seemingly salivating as it turned its non-existent gaze to his genitalia. Then, in a visual flickering flutter that precisely matched the obnoxiously loud shudder of sounds, the demon wriggled and wormed its way up Mr. C.'s vulnerable body. Until, it finally reached his neck, where it wrapped its slimy, shimmering indigo-black extremities.

Without warning, a surge of pus-colored ectoplasm was discharged from the entity and injected into Mr. C.'s frontal lobe; the demon dissolved into a mud-colored mess. It was like helplessly witnessing a spiritual lobotomy of a once fiery soul. Something in his exhausted eyes became a bit twisted; there was one final stellar screech emitted from some other space or paralleled plane of existence. In that moment, Emerlyn knew what she had to do.

"Emerlyn!" Mr. C. snapped his fingers before her eyes. "Are you okay? Talk to me!"

"Yea, Mr. C., I'm sorry. I know this probably won't make a lot of sense to you, but I need to tell you something," Emerlyn paused, knowing she had to choose her words carefully as she allowed the gravity of a necessary deception to wash over her aching heart. "I can't fully explain it, but I've identified the Dream Demon's next target."

"What? Who is it Em?" Mr. C.'s eyes widened with fear and anger. "Well? Spit it out! Who is it?"

"It's you, Mr. C. It's already infecting you. I can see what it's doing to you, but I know how to fix it! We can still stop this thing, together." As Emerlyn spoke the words, she began to cry. Her tears had more to do with the truths she omitted than the lies she told, though.

Mr. C. put his back against the cold wall and slid down to sit on the floor. "How? I feel so helpless against this thing."

"The answer lies beneath the old tree in the hollow. We have to go back to the--"

"The secret chamber?" Mr. C. interrupted.

"Yea, how'd you know?" Emerlyn wiped the tears from her face revealing a look of perplexity.

"At first, it was difficult to believe Thomas's story about a demonic chamber beneath the bleeding tree, but then I saw what my wife was up to. She'd been doing some digging through the old records in our library. I think she knew more about that damned place than any of us. No wonder she hated my dumb ghost stories. I can't believe she ever put up with me." Mr. C. hid his face in his palms as he sniffled. "And then I saw a book at Paige's house. That's when I knew everything you kids told me at the hospital was true."

"Mr. C., there's more." Emerlyn strained with every fiber in her being as she fought to hide the truth behind her lying eyes. "We have to go there, now. The deadline to save you is 3:33 am."

"An angelic hour or the true witching hour?" Mr. C asked as he slowly rose to his feet.

"Truth be told, it's a bit of both. Good and evil are more intertwined than I'd ever imagined, Mr. C."

"Yea, I'm starting to sense that. I'll tell Jack we're just going for a drive." Mr. C. cleared his throat and straightened his posture. "I want to keep him far away from this thing. Em, if anything happens to me, if this shit goes sideways, I need you to tell him that I love him. I need you to let him know that he's not alone. Emerlyn, he's lost everyone he loves. If he loses me, too, you'll have to take care of him. He's got no one else to turn to."

"Mr. C., I will never let anything happen to Jack. I swear it. We can stop this thing tonight, but we have to go now." Emerlyn whimpered beneath her promise. It was a pact she took to heart, a sacred oath that she would never, ever violate.

"Just one more thing," Mr. C. paused. "How do you think it'll try to take me out?"

Emerlyn's eyes watered as she slowly touched the tips of her trembling fingers to the purple and rust-colored bruises around her throat.

"Oh...I see." Mr. C. turned away from Emerlyn. Each reluctant step he took landed with the heavy thud of a hammer, driving another nail into his own coffin. He could feel it burning deep inside his chest. He could see his fate reflected in Emerlyn's defeated eyes.

Chapter 23

Emerlyn and Mr. C. panted as they pushed the stone altar from the secret entrance of the undercroft. The small wooden shack was harder to find in the cover of darkness. Emerlyn barely recognized it. She glanced one last time at the pagan symbols of protection that were awash with silver moonlight before entering the passage. Mr. C. took the first step down the gritty, stone stairs lifting his flashlight and peering into the tunnel. Normally, he'd have his gun in hand; but he knew earthly weapons would do him no favors in this place. He scoffed at the devilish colors, terrifying textures, and crudely carved walls.

"I know this goes without saying Em, but I hate everything about this fucking place." He glanced at his watch. "It's 3AM Emerlyn. I hope it's not much further. We're running low on time."

"It's not far, Mr. C." Emerlyn worked hard to hide the massive lump of rotting guilt lodged in her aching throat.

In spite of the cold, her palms and armpits were sweaty; and she often had to remind herself just to breathe. She pondered sinister scenarios inside her befuddled brain. The thought of drugging Mr. C. with the pills in her pocket must have crossed Emerlyn's mind a thousand times. She knew what she had to do, where she had to do it, but she'd not yet figured out the how of it.

As the two ventured deeper into the grotty bowels of Satan, they finally reached the rubble. For Mr. C. it felt like the point of no return.

"I'm assuming you know something I don't, because this looks like a dead end."

"It's a dead end; but shine your flashlight over here, along this wall," Emerlyn replied nervously. "Max leaned somewhere around here and fell into the chamber. If we push hard enough on the stones, I'm sure we can find the trigger mechanism."

Mr. C. 's face was illuminated by the splash of light that reflected from the red walls. In the crimson hue, Emerlyn could see his soul dying from the parasitic demon. A spiritual decay had set in, and Mr. C.'s once powerful presence was now but a meek mumble, a mere whisper of a man. Still, he pushed along the wall with all his might.

"Here, it's moving!" A stone depressed revealing a hidden cavity riddled with familiar demonic enns that Mr. C. had studied in demonology books. The same devilish mysticism that had temporarily bewitched Emerlyn's mind now had its black-hearted hold on him. "Fascinating…" Mr. C. muttered as he walked beneath the creepy, fingerlike roots that reached from above and clutched the cryptic carvings of the chamber down below. Suddenly, he snapped out of the unholy trance and turned towards Emerlyn who stood nervously at the hole-and-corner door. He pointed the blinding light into her eyes and removed his 10mm pistol from its holster.

"I know what you intend to do, Em. Someone much wiser tried to warn me of this place of death. As I said before, I saw the sketches near my wife's lifeless corpse. Then, at Paige's house, I thumbed through that strange book of spells. There, I saw mention of a ceremony taking place beneath the bleeding tree with no alternative to being buried alive; and I can feel a black sickness brewing inside me. I know on which side of that door I belong."

"Mr. C., what are you saying?" Emerlyn could no longer hide the tears in her voice.

"I heard the rattling of those pills in your pocket. At first, I thought you might spike my drink or drug me some other way. Now that we're here, I'm not sure what you're planning. Frankly, I don't think you even have a plan," Mr. C. continued to hold the light in one hand and his gun in the other.

"You have to understand. There is no other way." Emerlyn shielded her eyes from the light as she continued to cry.

"I understand, Em. It's a dead end for me, now. I know how this goes." A single, cold tear fell from Mr. C.'s tired eyes as he stepped forward and handed the light and pistol to Emerlyn. "Here, take these. You'll be needing them on your way out of here. You know the drill. There's a round in the chamber."

"I don't want to leave you, Mr. C.; I don't want to go!" Emerlyn wept; and her knees became weak, involuntarily bending as she stumbled in place.

A burning surge of despair seemed to sear through the very marrow of her bones. Emerlyn pointed the gun away from Mr. C. and wrapped her arms around him, hugging him with all her might. It was mostly a genuine moment of affection, but partially a moment of opportunity for Emerlyn to seize the grimoire page from his pocket. After all, she'd made a deal with Lucifer to destroy it, to end this forever. She could not let Mr. C. die in vain.

"Em, I need you and Jack to take care of each other. You're both so strong. I love you like a daughter. Now, I need you to get the hell out of here before it's too late." Mr. C. glanced at his watch. "It's 3:30."

Emerlyn reluctantly nodded and slowly backed out of the chamber. She kept her eyes on Mr. C. hoping he'd stop her, hoping he'd find another way to beat the demon. There was nothing but dead air between them. She took a deep breath, then sealed the secret passage behind her.

Without warning, the entire tunnel system began to quake and crumble. Emerlyn could hear Mr. C. screaming from within the demonic cavern. The veinlike roots from the tree that cradled the cavity seemed to throb through the walls of the undercroft. She couldn't imagine what sorts of horrid things were happening to him as the curse of the Dream Demon was slowly undone. Instinctively, Emerlyn picked up the gun and flashlight from the faulting ground beneath her and darted towards the stone stairs. As she ran, the swaying flashlight revealed the startling sight of serpents slithering at her feet. Emerlyn gasped as she felt fluttering bats clawing at her hair, saw spiders dangling from the collapsing vermillion ceiling, and heard rats screaming for their dear lives.

Worst of all were the poor victims' souls, quickly crawling through the chamber walls in shame. They'd escaped the prison of the dybbuk but feared the nightmarish things that might await them in Hell. First, Amelia and Holcomb scrambled past Emerlyn's heels on all fours, a crippling side-effect of spirits trapped and contorted inside the binds of an inhuman entity for over a century. Emerlyn could swear she heard Amelia whisper in sorrowful gratitude as she scurried past. At that moment, Emerlyn was reassured that she was not an evil witch but a foolish girl that paid dearly for her mistakes. There were several other spirits that crept by like crooked little things whose identities would remain unknown.

Then, there was Mrs. C., bewildered and baffled by her circumstances. It was such a cruel irony to serve as the end of a legend she loathed with all her heart. Shortly after, Deputy Huey sprinted out the chamber with Paige lying in his arms. Emerlyn continued to race towards the exit, and she reached out in vain as the two scrambled by at lightning speed. To say it wasn't painful to see Paige that way would be a blatant lie. What she felt was beyond the human understanding of pain and torment, but the worst was yet to come.

Finally, there was Thomas holding the hand of his little brother, Max. Something immediately shattered inside Emerlyn's heart, and she paused beneath the crumbling catacomb. Time stood still as the three locked eyes. For a moment, the cacophony of chaos and devilry disappeared. No words were exchanged because words were not enough, not even close. Their eyes told a story that a lifetime of syllables could never encapsulate. Emerlyn knew that this was Lucifer's way of holding up his end of the bargain.

A sudden sound of rapidly flowing water filled the air. Emerlyn turned to see a monstrous river of blood rushing towards her. She ran as faster than she'd ever run before, but the crimson tide was steadily gaining on her. She dug deeper, quickly depleting the last of her energy reserves. With one final push, Emerlyn reached the pale moonlight at the foot of the stone stairs. She paused and took a deep breath of fresh air near the top of the staircase. The crimson red river pooled in around her feet, then vanished. Alas, she could breathe. Emerlyn's heart beat so hard beneath her breast that she could feel her eyes pulsate with every thunderous thump. Her body was weak and her mind weary, but it felt like it was finally over.

Unfortunately, the old wooden shack that surrounded her had suffered too much structural damage from the violent tremors below. A large beam splintered with an ear-splitting crack and fell onto Emerlyn's head, violently knocking her to the cold, unforgiving ground. Everything went black. There were no ghosts or ghouls, no angels or demons, only a placid plane of darkness that went on and on forever. And further, still.

Chapter 24

"Oh no! How did she get out?" the voice of a teenage boy eagerly inquired.

"Is that it? Did someone save her?" a young girl pleaded.

"Those are excellent questions...that you'll have to ask your mother!"

"Jack! What did you tell them?" Emerlyn asked as she entered the kitchen. "I come bearing gifts for my two favorite chime children!" She stood near the table dressed as a witch, holding a black cauldron of candy.

"Mom, we're not kids anymore!" the boy exclaimed.

"Thomas, you'll always be my child." Emerlyn winked as she tilted her witch hat and pushed the bucket of treats towards her son. "And Paige, that goes for you, too! No more growing up! That's an order!"

"I second that motion!" Jack laughed.

"So Jack, what exactly did you tell our children?" Emerlyn narrowed her eyes.

"Oh, you know. I just kind of explained the grimoire from the hollow and why it's so important for us to find the remaining books. . ." Jack's eyes wandered around the room as they avoided contact with his wife.

"And?" Emerlyn persisted.

"And maybe, I told them a little about Amelia and stuff." Jack cleared his throat. "And how their grandmother is sort of a descendant of a witch?"

"Jack! Come on, I thought we agreed not to tell them that story! It's so graphic!" Emerlyn frowned.

"Sorry, Hunnie! I left out the worst parts. I promise! Sooner or later, we're gonna need their help. I'm getting too old for this stuff." Jack reached into the candy cauldron and snickered at his daughter.

Emerlyn turned and walked towards the open window, her gothic Victorian gown floating just behind her. She stared into the twilight as if she were searching for something. Truth be told, she'd never stopped searching for the other books of which Lucifer spoke. They'd haunted her dreams ever since; hovering over her like a heavy, black void while she slept.

Part of her died that Halloween, dangling from the rafters above her grandmother's old rocking chair. She could still hear Mr. C. screaming in agony as the demonic leech was ripped from his body and severed from his essence. She could still smell the odor of death that puffed in putrid black clouds as she torched the grimoire page in a pile filled with every facsimile of demonic literature she could find. The memories were like a poison that festered in Emerlyn's soul, a blot of ink that permanently stained her lifeblood and all that she loved. In the back of her mind, she wondered if she even had a soul at all. After being touched by Lucifer, Emerlyn wondered how much of her life was her own. The celestial never so much as whispered to her again, but she feared what wicked nightmares might await her after death.

Sensing her heavy heart, Jack joined his wife near the window. He, too, felt the insidious infection of darkness, left behind by an irreplaceable loss of life. Jack took a deep breath to calm himself and placed his arm around Emerlyn's shoulders.

"It's beautiful. Isn't it?" he said.

A cool breeze crept in, and a blanket of shimmering stars began to pierce the blued, nighttime sky. The last few rays of fading light burned a deep red hue beneath the horizon of the setting sun, casting three large pyramid-shaped silhouettes that towered over the arid Egyptian landscape like gods.

"It's one of the most beautiful things I've ever seen," Emerlyn whispered as the wind gently swept across the dunes like waves in a vast ocean of golden sand.

"It's not even close for me," Jack replied as he hugged his wife and turned to look at their children.

Emerlyn smiled, leaning into Jack's warm embrace. "Thomas. Paige. Do you really want to know who saved me that night?"

"Yes! Tell us, Mom!" the two clamored.

"It was your Grandpa Carter. Somehow, someway, he lifted me out of that rubble and breathed new life into me. Your grandfather had a will that transcended death." Emerlyn's eyes watered as she continued to smile.

"My ole man was too righteous for Hell and too stubborn for Heaven. I have a sneaking suspicion that he's still around here somewhere, watching over the two of you." Jack's chest swelled with a bit of pride and sorrow; he took another deep breath, then let it go. Once more, Emerlyn turned to the open window. She grabbed the squeaky wooden shutters and paused just before closing them. A cold gust of wind left her arms riddled with goosebumps, but there was something else. Something called to her from the darkness.

'Emerlyn...Wake up.'

FIN

In loving memory of
Troy Pelsia

INTO THE HOLLOW

"Amelia was very real, as real as the oldest tree in the hollow that still stands near the ruins of the church. People say that on the days leading up to Halloween, the barrier between our world and the spirit realm grows thin, her soul becomes restless, and she is able to cross over..."

It's the night before Halloween in the year 2020, and all Hell is breaking loose. After hearing a ghostly tale of witches, cults, and curses from his father, Jack and his horror fanatic friends venture deep into the haunted hollow in search of paranormal evidence. With high school graduation and the pressures of college looming just around the corner, the teens are determined to escape the everyday monstrosities of society and have the scariest All Hallows' Eve of their lives. The veil is thin, the moon is full, and there's no telling what wicked wonders await them.

CPSIA information can be obtained
at www.ICGtesting.com
Printed in the USA
BVHW070411050920
588151BV00001B/28

9 781728 368047